The Sunflower Connection

The Sunflower Connection

D. C. Walsh

Published by Tablo

Published in 2021 by Tablo Publishing.

Publisher and wholesale enquiries: orders@tablo.io

20 21 22 23 LSC 10 9 8 7 6 5 4 3 2 1

In loving memory of
Dad & Hayley.

Even in our darkest moments
the universe fills the sky
with sights that reveal glimpses of heaven.

CHAPTER ONE

Leon normally avoided cities. Crowds in general were a chronic source of irritation, let alone swarms of goggle-eyed sightseers like the ones that flocked to the Queensland coast year-round. Tourists were more annoying than blowflies, the way they flitted around the place spreading their foreign germs. And it was even worse since that rotten virus hit.

Outback towns were more to his liking, small communities you could only get to by driving backside-numbing days along monotonously straight strips of red-dirt road. People in the bush were nosy numbats, but at least there weren't so many of them. He'd already been in Aurora Waters far longer than he would have liked, and if he wasn't on his way by the end of March, someone else would end up paying for it.

He parked the stolen Mazda under the umbrella shade of a splashy Poinciana, glad of some relief from the blazing autumn sun. The sprawling branches covered with fern-like leaves, would screen out the worst of the midday heat, and keep him from baking like a loaf of damper in a camp oven while he waited. Even at that time of year, the sun managed to pack a red-hot punch, and any relief was better than nothing.

Hunched low in the seat, with a curtain of feathery foliage for camouflage, he kept an eye on the girl as she stepped out onto the road. The blustery easterly whipped her hair around her face, and before she could catch it, her skirt blew up in a sudden gust, exposing long, shapely legs.

The unexpected glimpse of lace edged panties dragged his mind to the time he'd watched her on the beach. Most of the other dolls on the coast baked themselves to a crisp on the white sand every day—but not her. She lathered herself in sunscreen and covered up with a hat and one of those sarong things when she wasn't in the water. Thinking about the way she rubbed lotion over her curvy body got his blood going, and he imagined what it would be like to get his hands on her. He wasn't a patient man, and it helped him tolerate all the waiting around.

Despite his hurry, it was too risky to show his face at the girl's apartment block, especially with that hulking security guard coming and going at all hours. The dozy suburban street where her family lived was a far safer bet. Even on Sunday, the renovated show homes that lined the street, were as lifeless as a waterhole in the middle of a drought. Lucky for him, the Glass family were as docile as a mob of sheep and almost as dopey. A few more minutes dogging jittery Gemma should be enough to see the job done.

There was no boyfriend on the scene, or at least none that he'd noticed. Waste of a good body, but it was one less complication. Not that the girl would be much of an obstacle. She didn't seem to know what day it was half the time, and he wondered if all the medical treatment had caused permanent damage. Not the type of scatterbrain he wanted to pin his future on, but he had little choice in the matter.

He checked himself out in the rear-view mirror. He was a good-looking rooster, an edge that had proven useful in the past. He'd never had any problems getting sheilas to throw themselves at him. The beard and shaggy hair had taken a bit of getting used to, especially with the humidity on the coast, but he couldn't take the risk of anybody spotting him. He would get rid of it once he was far enough out of town. By then a dye job and stubble would do the trick.

He watched her walk around to the passenger side door.

The whole operation would have been so much easier if her old Hyundai had broken down along the highway. He could have offered her a lift, or a hand with repairs. Any excuse to get up close and personal without drawing attention to himself. The rusty heap of shit was almost as old as she was, but it hadn't missed a beat in the three miserable days he'd been following her, and he wished he'd sabotaged the bloody thing days ago.

After fiddling around with something on the front passenger seat for a minute, she straightened up with a bunch of scraggly flowers in her arms. Then out of the blue, she turned in his direction.

Hoping she hadn't seen him, he ducked behind the dashboard.

He was wound up tight, and when his hands stiffened around the steering wheel, he ordered himself to take it easy. He didn't want to go off half-cocked. If he was going to make his play before she went inside, he had to keep his wits about him. Flexing his fingers to release the tension, he wiped his palms along his pants legs. Once he had himself in check, his right hand shifted to the door handle and he slipped out of the car.

Fuck! He couldn't believe his bad luck. Someone was keeping tabs on her from one of the upstairs windows.

Although he was positive he could take care of her family if push came to shove, another mistake would likely be the end of him. He wanted to go for it anyway, but he couldn't afford to blow the whole operation when he was so close. His rage flared at the delay, and fighting to keep his anger under control, he vented his frustration on the car door; slamming it so hard, the bang echoed down the street.

He was sick and tired of all this cloak and dagger garbage, and he didn't intend to stand for much more of it. There had to be an easier way.

He would hang around until she came out, then after he took care of business, he would treat himself to a little bonus. She owed it to him for putting him to so much trouble, making him wait around in the stinking heat and getting him all hot and bothered. Besides, she could do with a bit of loosening up. It was probably just what the doctor ordered. And if she didn't give him what he wanted...

His greasy fingers tightened around the steering wheel again.

CHAPTER TWO

Reaching down to the passenger seat to grab the sunflowers, Gemma froze like a mannequin in a department store window when an anonymous hand reached out of nowhere to pluck a perfect bloom from the middle of her bouquet. Sensing that it wasn't one of her cheap sunflowers at risk, she watched—spellbound—as deft fingers crushed a few flawless petals.

The ominous vision dissolved as suddenly as it had appeared, and there was no way to tell whether it had been an omen or a premonition. She could only hope her day wouldn't get any more bizarre.

The leafy housing estate where her family lived was eerily quiet. There was no blaring music, children had disappeared from manicured lawns, not even birdsong penetrated the dense atmosphere. The only sound was an ambient murmuring drone that sent chills up her spine. At first she thought it was traffic noise, but the rhythm was more organic, and even as she considered its origin, the volume increased.

A sweeping glance around the deserted street convinced her there was no immediate threat, but when a car door slammed nearby, it set her nerves on edge, and she raced up the drive of her parents' house.

The front door was wide open, with only an unlocked security screen protecting her family from potential intruders. A blue bridal garter draped provocatively over the door handle, reminded her why she was there, and despite the uneasy feeling that had been haunting her for days, she shrugged off her mood and thought about the task ahead.

Following the scent of blood orange from one of her mother's candles, she found her arranging furniture in the large, open-plan living area at the rear of the house.

"I didn't hear you come in love." Kristin Glass clattered over imitation marble tiles on hazardously high heels, to place a delicate peck on her daughter's cheek. Even with the additional height afforded by the shoes, she needed to reach. "Glad to see you remembered the sunflowers. It's always handy to have an extra bit of luck on our side. Have you been busy?"

Gemma laid the flowers on the island bench that separated the kitchen from the rest of the casual living area. "The website's been steady. No big jobs with the agency lately though. A few pieces from the new lingerie range would be nice."

"We'll see. It depends how well you perform." Her mother aimed a sideways glance at her as she continued the preparation for the party.

Although Gemma knew she was only teasing, she felt the pressure anyway. "Is Angela excited?"

"She's thrilled about the party, and even more ecstatic about the engagement. She's been single for years… like someone *else* we know." Her mother sent another sidelong glance her way. "She met Matt online. Who would have thought?"

"Good for her. I spend enough time online as it is. I prefer to meet people the old-fashioned way."

"And how's that strategy working out for you? I hear Matt is a real catch. Goes to show you should never lose hope. I'm giving them lingerie as an engagement gift. He'll be more grateful than Angela when he sees it."

"I'm sure it will come in very handy on the wedding night. Where's Dad?" It was time to change the subject before her mother tried to talk her into downloading Angela's dating app.

"Do you really need to ask? He's at the sports club. No way he would hang around the house for one of my parties."

"Will Naomi be here today?"

"It wouldn't be any fun without her." A crooked smile skewed the corners of her mother's fuchsia tinted lips. "But at least if Doug's not here, I won't need to keep such a close eye on her with the champagne."

"He's not exactly thrilled with what either of us do for a living, is he?"

"As long as he doesn't have to be here, he can block it out and pretend it's not happening. Besides, he gets to admire the merchandise in private."

Gemma pretended to gag. "I really didn't need to hear that. As if I don't have enough disturbing pictures crashing my skull uninvited."

"You're old enough not to be offended by the idea of a mature couple enjoying themselves in the bedroom my darling."

"Give me a break. I'm already dealing with enough issues to keep me in therapy for another ten years."

"You've always been such a sensitive little thing." She ran scented fingers over Gemma's fine stream of ash-brown hair, tucking a wayward tendril behind her ear. "Comes with the territory I suppose. As for your father, he worries about you. We both do. I'd better keep moving, the girls will be here soon."

"You're the little one. I've been head and shoulders over you for years. I'll put the flowers in a vase. Are you sure there's nothing else you need me to do? What about the spare bedroom?"

"It's ready to go. Once I get a few drinks into the partygoers, they'll be keen to try on all the pretties."

"Is the gremlin locked in his dungeon?" She was only half joking.

"If only it was legal to lock him in. He knows to stay in there until the party's over. Not that he comes out very often anyway. If he goes anywhere near the change room again, he's in serious trouble."

Gemma chose a vase for the sunflowers from her mother's collection. It wasn't as extravagant as the one she had seen in her vision, but it would have to do. It fit right in with the faux velvet throws and gaudy silk scarves draped over the furniture.

"What do you think about the decor? I thought I'd go for a combination of boudoir chic and fortune teller's caravan."

"You've been running the business long enough to know what you're doing. It's not my taste, but I suppose it serves the purpose."

Her mother seemed pleased with herself, and once the bubbly started to flow, it tended not to matter anyway. A combination of lamplight and scented candles softened the effect, and an assortment of even more questionable props would be brought out later, when everyone had loosened up with a champagne or two.

"It's not about taste, my darling. It's about mystery and intrigue… and fun. You're so uptight, you must take after your father."

The doorbell interrupted their conversation, chiming to the triumphal tune of Here Comes the Bride.

That was her cue to exit, and while her mother added the final touches to her merchandise display, she fled down the hall to answer the door.

Kristin's best friend was first to arrive, greeting Gemma with an affectionate hug and the warmth of a beloved aunt. "Hello beautiful, fancy meeting you here. You look well."

Although she loved Laura, Gemma cringed inwardly at the familiar phrase. It not only implied that she had gained weight, but it also reminded her of her illness, and either way she couldn't win.

"Before we join the party," Laura said, "I thought I'd try to jump the queue for a private reading. Are you free now?"

"Of course, anything for you. Besides, that's what I'm here for."

As a long-standing family friend, Laura had provided invaluable comfort and support during the emotionally draining years of her illness, and she would never refuse a special request from her. Resting one hand on her silk clad arm, Gemma relaxed and tried to concentrate. In the darkness behind her eyes, bright spots of light that usually danced in haphazard array, joined together to create a fuzzy impression.

"How many children does Heidi have now?" she asked.

"I knew it, Lee's having another baby, isn't she? Will it be a girl this time? I've always wanted a granddaughter."

"I can't tell you that, Heidi would kill me. I don't know how far in the future it is… they may not even know themselves yet. I don't want you to be disappointed if things don't turn out the way you expect. Remember there are no guarantees."

"Don't be so critical of yourself," Laura scolded her gently, "you've never let me down before. I'm going to be a grandmother again, how exciting. Thank you beautiful, you've made my day."

The next hour was a blur for Gemma. Her role was to mingle with the guests and perform impromptu clairvoyant readings while her mother tempted them with an array of food and drinks and an introduction to her latest lingerie range. At her request, Gemma's psychic interpretations included an occasional inventive scenario designed to boost sales.

As part of the fun, the bride-to-be was repeatedly urged to show off the items she planned to wear on her wedding night. She may have eventually agreed if not for an unexpected interruption.

Kristin left the room to answer the door, only to return soon afterwards with a police officer in tow. Girlish laughter subsided to breathless giggles and there was a sudden rush to recover missing clothing items.

"Angela, I'm so sorry. This police officer is here to deliver some very bad news."

"Angela Martin?" Stern eyes roamed the room, lingering in simmering intensity on every face.

Kristin pushed Angela forward.

"Ms. Martin, I'm sorry to inform you that your days of freedom are over. My name is Constable Carl, and you are under arrest for crimes against single men everywhere."

The pretend police officer's face erupted in an impudent grin as he removed his cap and floated it up into the air toward the enthralled audience. Sliding behind Angela, he seized her hips and guided her towards a waiting chair. Once she was in position, he grasped the front of his shirt with both hands and wrenched his costume away, baring a smoothly tanned body, rippling with bulging muscles.

There was an audible gasp from the crowd, and with all eyes trained on Angela and her handsome seducer, she immediately turned a similar shade of red to one of Kristin's flashy throws.

As raunchy music blasted out around the room, Carl's erotic gyrations—of which Angela reaped most benefit—prompted facial expressions among the goggle-eyed women ranging from awe to awkwardness. The rapt audience offered enthusiastic encouragement for his efforts in the form of shouts and whistles, while the practically naked entertainer thrust his lascivious hips in time to the music and moved the rest of his meticulously sculpted body in ways designed to make half the onlookers blush and the other half drool with desire.

Gemma rated an entertaining male stripper as much as anyone, and while her appreciative eyes were riveted to Carl's pumped-up body, her usually restrained mouth dropped open of its own accord at some of his more exotic moves.

Her attention only wavered when an erratic movement in the corner of the crowded room dragged her gaze away from his provocative performance. On the floor against the back wall was a model racing car, and although it was partly obscured by curtains and preoccupied bodies, she was sure it hadn't been there earlier.

Following a hunch, she marched up the stairs like a stealth bomber on a mission and barged into her little brother's bedroom without knocking.

Lucas and James were both there. They had been friends since their first day of school and if Lucas was home, James usually wasn't far away. Lucas was rolling around in hysterics on his bed, and when he saw her, he jumped up and made a dash for his desk.

"It's too late. I'm onto you," she told him. Before his laptop screen went blank, she copped an eyeful of Carl's thong-clad backside, thrusting and clenching in glorious high definition.

"Don't tell Mum. I was only mucking around. There's nothing else to do. It's boring around here." His cheeks flushed pink beneath their freckles.

Lucas was a nerd. It wasn't difficult to work out there was a miniature camera attached to the toy car. He was clearly satisfying his teenage curiosity (or other urges), and she wondered whether he was more interested in Constable Carl, the lingerie, or the women who had been demonstrating it. She made a mental note not to burst into his room unannounced in future. As obnoxious as he was, her little brother was growing up.

"Where did you get the equipment? And how did you get the car in there—you sneaky Houdini? I swear it wasn't there earlier in the afternoon."

"Remote control. I waited until everyone was pissed before I sent it in."

She noted the lopsided grin that surfaced whenever he thought he had gotten the better of tech illiterate adults. "I'm not pissed, and neither is Mum. We were distracted by the arrival of… the entertainer, not to mention some of the appliances that Angela received as gifts. You weren't watching while Angela unwrapped her presents were you?"

"It's not as if I haven't seen that sort of stuff before," he sniggered. "There's this thing called the internet you know."

"You haven't explained where you got the camera." She used her most intimidating big sister voice. "Harvey gave it to you, didn't he?"

"He said not to tell you."

"I'm going to have a word with him about this next time I see him. Mum and Dad would go berserk if they knew you had been hanging around Harvey behind their backs."

"Don't say anything, I won't do it again. I promise." Lucas always vowed to behave whenever he got caught out.

If he stayed out of serious trouble and didn't continue his involvement with her enigmatic boss, she concluded it was only natural for a teenage boy to be curious. "Make sure you erase all traces of Constable Carl right now. I'm going to impound your devious toy, and if I catch you doing anything like this again, I'm telling Mum and Dad."

"I'm putting a lock on my door."

On her way out, Gemma scolded James with a withering stare as well, even though he had no influence with Lucas. Once she would have relied on him to help curb her disobedient brother's more outlandish pranks. Sadly, those days were over.

"And you owe me one," she added as an afterthought.

The party was almost over when she returned downstairs, and she helped her mother see off the last of her guests.

"Where did you get to? You missed the best part—the sales."

"I looked in on Lucas to make sure he's staying out of trouble." She checked the spot where the car had been, but it was gone.

"Thanks for going along with my plan, love. The way you described those saucy visions made all the difference to sales. We'll have to put our heads together to come up with some new ideas. We wouldn't want our regular customers to become blasé."

"I'm not comfortable misleading people like that Mum. It's dishonest."

"Nonsense. Everyone knows it's only a bit of fun. They love it. Toni was thrilled when you told her where to find her watch. Her bedroom will get a thorough going over now, in more ways than one. It's sure to be hidden away in there somewhere. If she doesn't find it, she'll blame the cleaner for swiping it anyway. The party turned out to be a nice little money earner, all in the name of love. Well done, my darling."

"She would have found it without my help if it's where I think it is. But she seemed happy."

"If everyone is happy, it means more profit for me. And no one would have bought all my fabulous merchandise if you hadn't hinted how much it would improve their love lives. From what I know of those girls, a little fantasy is all the action most of them see these days. Let's hope the new lingerie will do the trick."

Gemma tried to see the creative use of her ability as light-hearted entertainment rather than blatant deception. "I suppose so. Angela seemed less embarrassed by the end."

"There was no doubt she was ecstatic about my surprise. It was the second-best part, or should I say parts?" A suggestive smile left no doubt about her meaning. "You missed most of it. Why were you gone so long?"

"Not that I didn't appreciate Carl's dance moves, but Lucas and I were having a brother-sister bonding session."

Her mother's heavily arched brows became even more prominent. "So, there *is* a first time for everything. I never thought I'd see the day."

"Besides, I don't like to be reminded of what I'm missing out on."

"Oh love, you'll find the right man one day. For all you know, he could be waiting for you right around the next corner. Then again, I suppose if anyone would know—you would."

CHAPTER THREE

Gemma's concentration was as erratic as her bank account, (not that a minor brain fog was significantly different to her usual scattered reality). The readings she had performed at the party had drained her energy levels, plus she was starving. If she hadn't been so preoccupied with finding out what Lucas was up to with his super-spy prank, she would have raided her mother's pantry when she'd had the chance.

After leaving her parents' house, she took a slight detour off Marine Highway, and pulled over near a small group of shops on Arbor Road. There was no one around, and a quick visit to Bernie's Bargain Food Mart, provided her with enough food to see her through another twenty-four hours. A loaf of bread, a carton of milk, and a frozen dinner would tide her over until she had the time and energy for a longer shopping expedition. They weren't called convenience stores for nothing!

On the way back to her car with the groceries, the air was charged with the sound of a low hum, like bees buzzing around a hive. The light was dimmer too, as if an afternoon storm had rolled across while she was inside. Checking above her head, she noted there wasn't a cloud in the sky, let alone a swarm of bees.

After a few more steps, a wave of nausea hit her, and although wishful thinking tried to convince her that it was only exhaustion, instinct screamed that something bad was about to happen.

She picked up her pace, but it made no difference.

Mid-stride, a pair of gorilla arms caught her from behind, stopping her dead in her tracks. Before she could call for help, a rough hand clamped over her mouth, smashing her lips against her teeth. She tasted his sweat on her tongue, and the reek of it lodged in the back of her throat, making it hard to breathe through the stench.

When her revolted stomach tried to throw up in her mouth, she dropped the bag of groceries and clawed at the hairy mitt over her face. Being a nervous nail biter, her stubby fingernails weren't long enough to scratch off a layer of dirt, let alone his grimy skin, and it turned out to be a useless strategy.

"Stop squirming or I'll break your scrawny neck." The raspy voice was coarse and menacing, and the pressure of his arms demonstrated that he would have little trouble making good on his threat. He dragged her effortlessly, and for all the difference her struggles made, she could have been a life-sized doll stuffed with cotton wool.

While he hauled her backwards, her bulging eyes swept left and right in a frantic search for help.

Zoning in on a tour bus parked along the street, she watched the doors open and potential salvation emerge, in the form of a group of energetic teenage boys. Talking and laughing among themselves, they burst onto the footpath, focused on their destination. Dressed in identical muddy brown polo shirts, they charged along the concrete pavement, oblivious to their surroundings, reminding her of a herd of wild animals stampeding towards a watering hole.

To get their attention, she waved her arms around like a teenage girl at a boy band concert.

They didn't appear to notice her, and the move only provoked the dirt-bag into crushing her even harder against his repulsive body.

Thinking her gamble hadn't paid off, she was convinced her one hope of rescue was passing her by, until a couple of the boys stumbled onto her spilled groceries. When they stopped to take a closer look, two pairs of curious eyes turned in her direction. Seeing her predicament, it dawned on them what type of trouble she was in, and their bubbly chatter switched to shouts of anger.

With arms flailing the air as if trying to scare away a vicious dog, they raced to her rescue.

Seeing the two boys coming to her aid, a rush of adrenaline nudged Gemma's fear out of the way and she lashed out impulsively with a sharp backwards kick. The jarring impact of her heel connecting with a bony shin, sent a stab of pain through her foot, and a blast of filthy language flying over her head. Her captor relaxed his hold in the confusion, and she wrenched free of his grasp. Part-running and part-falling, she lunged awkwardly towards the approaching youths.

The remainder of the group caught up with them soon afterwards, and once she was safely surrounded, a tentative look reassured her that the thug was no longer in sight.

While helping her to retrieve the groceries, the boys tried to communicate with her in a foreign language that sounded like Japanese. It could have been Martian for all she cared. Their tone of voice and body language hinted that they were delighted with their contribution to her dramatic rescue, but it was difficult to make sense of anything with her heart still thudding like a kettledrum in her ears.

"My students are inquiring if you are hurt, Miss. You must excuse them. They are both excited about their adventure and concerned for your welfare. Are you injured?" The question came from a mature, English speaking version of the boys, who had appeared in their midst without her even noticing.

"I'm only in one piece thanks to them," she said, smiling and nodding. She wasn't sure how else to acknowledge their heroism when they didn't appear to understand her. "I don't know what I would have done if they hadn't come along when they did. Please tell them how grateful I am."

"They were merely performing their duty. That man is fortunate he drove away, my students would welcome an excuse to demonstrate their skill. Most of them are proficient in the art of Aikido."

Osaka High School was emblazoned across the front of the group's polo shirts. She hadn't noticed at first, because the words were obscured by high-tech cameras dangling around almost every student's neck.

Her brain was still scrambled, and she said the first thing that came into her head. "It must be a great school you have there. I should get them to show me some moves."

"Did you know that ruffian?" the teacher asked, ignoring her comment.

"I didn't see his face. I don't think so."

"Why was he assaulting you?"

"If you tell *me,* we'll both know."

He blinked. "I have no knowledge of why you were targeted in such a manner."

"Sorry. That's an expression. I have no idea either. It could have been a mugging. I didn't actually expect you to know."

"Ha! We should inform the authorities. Do you require a doctor?"

"No! No need for that. He's gone now. No harm done."

"In my country, it is customary to report such incidents to law enforcement. Are you certain you do not wish to call them?"

All she could think about was getting home to the safety of her apartment. "Thanks for the offer, but I'm sure you have better things to do. To tell the truth, I'm exhausted. The last thing I want to do is wait around for the police when there's nothing useful I can tell them anyway."

"Hmph."

His ambiguous guttural response hinted that he wasn't convinced, but he didn't stand in her way when she made a move to leave. After one last look around to ensure there was no further threat, she waved to her rescuers and drove off.

The apartment she had rented for the past three years was one of twelve, in a forty-year-old rendered brick box, a few blocks from the beach in the heart of Aurora Waters. Five minutes after leaving Bernie's, she turned down the paved driveway and parked in her designated spot underneath the building. The dirty yellow exterior had seen better days, but right then, it could have been a palatial coastal mansion and she wouldn't have been any more grateful to be home.

Prying rigid fingers from the steering wheel, she grabbed the sunflowers and groceries and climbed the internal stairs to the first floor. Wrapped up in her thoughts, she didn't notice a door slip open down the hall.

When a silent shadow exploded into her line of sight, she let out a startled squeak.

"What's wrong? Were you bitten by a cobra or something?" Lucky was dressed for work in his navy-blue security uniform.

"I was fine until you came out of nowhere and scared the fried ice cream out of me."

He shrugged. "Mmm… fried ice cream sounds good. Where else would I come from? That nowhere is where I live."

"I suppose you have a point. Anyway, I don't think we have cobras outside of zoos in Australia. If I'd been attacked by a snake, it would probably have been a red-bellied black or an eastern brown."

"I was joking about the cobra, but your face did remind me of my sister after one attacked her in the Jaipur market."

"Oh my God. Really?"

"No, it's another joke. I don't have a sister. I thought it would cheer you up. You better come in and tell us what's the matter. You look like you're gonna fall over."

Lucky's wife stood at the sink in the doll-sized kitchen that mirrored the one in her own apartment. "Why aren't you on your way to work, Ravnesh? What are you doing with Gemma? It's six o'clock."

Deera only called Lucky by his real name when she was angry with him or giving him the third degree about something. Gemma felt bad for getting him into trouble. "It's not his fault, he was only trying to help."

"She's upset my love. I thought you would want me to make sure she's OK."

"Then why didn't you say so?" Deera snapped off her rubber gloves and stepped out from behind the kitchen bench. Even while doing housework, she oozed good taste in a stylish floral dress. "What's wrong honey? You're shaking like a leaf. What happened?"

The alarm in her friend's voice dissolved the remains of Gemma's composure, and when she opened her mouth to reassure the couple, she burst into tears.

Deera wrapped a comforting arm around her heaving shoulders. "Take your time, there's no hurry. You're safe with us."

The attentive couple settled her on the sofa with a box of tissues in her lap.

"Feel better now?" Lucky asked once she had stopped sniffling.

"Uh huh, a bit. I guess I needed to get it out of my system."

"What happened? Did someone make you cry? Where are they?"

He sounded like he was ready to chase after the person who had upset her, and she pictured him hunting down the culprit to seek revenge on her behalf. She almost wished she could point him in the right direction.

"Some random grabbed me outside Bernie's. It was the human variety of snake—even worse than the real thing. He scared me half to death, before a group of kids chased him off."

"You should phone the police," Deera said. "Why would anyone want to attack you?"

"I haven't got a clue. I'm guessing it was a mugging. It was strange because he was dragging me towards his car. All I know is… he stank of B.O. and he was strong."

"He could have been taking you to his car so he could murder you— or rape you." Deera's face twisted with distaste as she suggested potential motives.

Gemma's mouth fell open and Lucky aimed a warning look at his wife. "Maybe it's a mistake. Maybe he thinks she's somebody else."

"I suppose it could have been a case of mistaken identity. That was my initial reaction as well." She worked through the possibilities. "It's a bit late to contact the police now, anyway."

"What if he tries again? You need police protection." Deera was insistent.

"Remember he only saw her from behind," Lucky pointed out, "but she should report it in case the villain attacks someone else."

"Oh, all right. I'll give them a call when I get home." She knew when she was outnumbered. "Thanks guys. I'm sorry to be such a pain. I feel like an idiot for breaking down like that."

"Don't be ridiculous. After what you went through, it's to be expected. Make sure you phone the police," Deera reminded her, "and remember, I'm only a few steps away if you need me."

Lucky escorted her to her apartment door and waited while she let herself in before rushing off to work.

When her hand reached for the light switch, something brushed up against her leg in the gloom, and she almost dropped the groceries again.

"Bobo, I wish you wouldn't do that." She flipped the switch and saw Bones at her feet. "Are you hungry? I didn't mean to be away so long."

The big ragdoll followed his usual routine, welcoming her home with a chorus of complaining cries and rumbling purrs.

She dumped the flowers and groceries in the kitchen and hoisted the heavy cat into her arms. A fluffy rug on the outside, with a solid lump of blubber on the inside, he was the ideal bundle for a cuddle. Resting her face against his velvet-soft fur, she was comforted by the consolation only an affectionate feline can provide.

"Where would I be without my precious fur baby?" she asked him with the crooning lullaby tone she used when she was happy with him. He answered her with a contented purr.

All Bones did was eat, sleep, and watch the world go by outside the apartment window. If he felt particularly adventurous, (which wasn't very often these days), he would wander into the garden or onto the balcony. He was already settled on his bed for a nap by the time her dinner was ready. A glass of white wine and a microwave dinner wasn't the most nutritious meal, but it did have a soothing effect on her shredded nerves.

After taking care of the dishes, she considered her priorities. Work with the agency had dwindled recently, and there were always bills to pay. A quick evaluation of the pros and cons and the decision was a foregone conclusion. Skimming her inbox, a request to find a ruby ring emerged as the most promising candidate for an easy win.

She studied the description of the ring and the photographs attached to the email to ensure she could identify the piece if she saw it. Then she closed her eyes.

The afterimage of the ring was clear at first, before gradually receding into the darkness. After it drifted away, all that remained was a speck of light in the furthest reaches of her perception. Through trial and error, she had learned how to follow the distant glow with her mind's eye, a sensation that felt like standing on a moving walkway inside a foggy tunnel. At the end of the ride, a sliver of shimmering vertical light identified the doorway to a different version of her own reality.

Through the thin, iridescent veil of light that constituted the barrier between the two dimensions, she watched a spaced-out youth pass a small item to a hawkish man behind a shop counter. As he evaluated it with an eyepiece, she noted both the fine gold setting and the sparkling gemstone closely matched the description of the missing ring. On the wall above one of the glass display cabinets that lined three sides of the overcrowded shop, was a sign advertising the conditions of sale for Perry's Pawnbrokers.

The discovery was potentially unwelcome news for her client, and Gemma wasn't sure if the information would lead to the ring's recovery, but it was better than nothing. At any rate, that was as far as she was prepared to go to earn a few dollars. She had only ventured through the mysterious portal once, and it was a mistake she had vowed never to repeat. No matter how many times she saw it, the parallel representation of her own reality continued to defy her understanding.

Replying to the email with a brief report, she wished the owner luck with recovering the ring and made a note to follow up with a standard customer feedback request.

CHAPTER FOUR

Bones tried to nudge her awake with his perfect pink toe beans, while his pitiful cries dragged her restless brain from the middle of a fitful dream.

Thanks to the previous day's events, she'd had a terrible night's sleep. But she knew there was little chance of more snooze time once the ruler of the universe decided he was starving. Nothing got in the way of her chubby ragdoll's need for food, and if she didn't satisfy his hunger quickly enough, he would resort to nipping her exposed flesh with his needle-sharp teeth. No matter how much she maneuvered to avoid him, the longer she delayed getting out of bed, the more aggressive his tactics would become.

Reluctantly caving in to his increasingly strident demands, she opened her bloodshot eyes to the glare of early morning sunshine filtered through translucent curtains. After a quick pit stop at the bathroom, she then plodded out to her dated kitchen with Bones snipping at her ankles to keep her moving.

From the cabinet above the stove that served as her pantry, she took the last remaining can of cat food, scooped the contents into a stainless-steel bowl and deposited it on the feeding mat that lived on the floor next to the kitchen bench. A piece of vegemite toast and a cup of coffee were all she could find for her own breakfast, and once the coffee kicked in, she was in a better frame of mind to assess her position.

Restocking the shelves would have to wait, and even then she may order online. The thought of venturing anywhere near a supermarket so soon after her ordeal made her stomach flip. The most tempting course of action was to lay low, forget the attack ever happened, and hope that it never happened again. Unfortunately, Deera would nag her to death if she didn't call the police.

Bec would know what to do. Her best friend had a way of dealing with garbage without getting covered in stink, a talent she had never quite mastered. Bec worked nights at the Meridian Casino, and given her own fragile emotional state, Gemma wasn't sure if she was prepared to handle the consequences of waking her grumpy friend too early.

Although anxious to speak to her, she employed a tactical delay, stalling for time by enjoying a leisurely shower and working on a few missing item requests. Not exactly sure whether there was a specific dress code for reporting a crime, after considering her available options, she settled for a pair of denim jeans and a white cotton tee in case a trip to the police station was unavoidable.

"Do you know what time it is? This better be an emergency." Bec's voice was thick with sleep when she answered her phone.

"Tell whoever it is to go away babe," a muffled voice complained in the background.

"Sorry if I disturbed your Dracula sleep or whatever else is going on there, but I need your opinion about something, and I couldn't wait any longer. It's about time you woke up and joined the land of the day walkers anyway."

"Give me half an hour," Bec said, "then feel free to join the party. In the meantime, I'll make my bed and get all the lumps out."

•••

When the elevator came to a stop at the thirty-fifth floor of The Bower on Baie, Gemma couldn't resist a longing look through the wide picture window at the surf end of the corridor. The high-rise location at Baie Sands had everything going for it, and she understood why Bec chose to live there. The view of turquoise water and golden sand, stretching as far as the eye could see to the east, was only eclipsed after dark, when millions of glittering lights created three-dimensional magic along the western horizon.

On the downside, drowning in debt only to pay someone else's mortgage wasn't Gemma's idea of sound financial strategy. Not that it would be within her budget anyway. She could barely keep up the rent on her rundown rabbit hole as it was. Bec's apartment was nice to visit, but she loved her homey hovel, with its dollar store decor and boring view. One day, if she was ever able to save enough money, she planned to own one just like it.

The door to apartment 3514 opened inwards at the exact same moment she raised her arm to knock, catching her off balance. As she clutched the air for support, a talking tornado snatched her up like a paper cut-out blowing in the wind.

"Careful love… wouldn't want you to hurt yourself. Call me…," he said, blowing a kiss over his shoulder.

After throwing a wink Gemma's way, he vanished.

He reminded her of someone, not that it mattered. If Bec ran true to form, it was unlikely she would run into him again any time soon.

"That was Connor. What do you think? Is he hot or what? He started work in the bar at the casino three weeks ago." Bec's sultry smile betrayed her satisfaction with her latest conquest.

"If you like the tall, muscle bound, tattooed type—then I suppose he's on point. What's his personality like?"

"Personality? Who needs one of those when you're built like that?" Bec laughed, sliding gracefully to the sofa. The way she smiled and stretched reminded Gemma of a human version of Bones, (only not as furry or fat).

"What's going on? Why so early? I haven't even had coffee yet."

"I need your advice on something."

"What else is new?"

Gemma braced herself. "Someone attacked me outside Bernie's yesterday afternoon." She blurted the words before she could change her mind.

"You're joking." Bec stiffened. "Why didn't you call me? I would have ditched work."

"Deera and Lucky helped me out, so there was no reason to bother you."

As Gemma described the attack, Bec's mood soured. "When they find him, I'm going to rip his head off. Better yet, I'll get Connor to rip his head off. Either way, he's a goner. What a dick." Her eyes blazed with lavender fire as she pretended to punch the lights out of a sofa cushion.

"I'm sure stuff like that happens every day. It all worked out in the end."

"What did the police say? I bet he's some sort of serial rapist or mugger. Has he attacked anyone else?"

"I'm on my way to Aurora Waters Police Station this afternoon. Do you want to keep me company?" So much for her plan to spend the afternoon on the beach.

"You're freaking hopeless, you should have called the police on the spot."

She didn't try to defend herself. Bec knew her too well.

"I can't believe you didn't report it yet. Damn right I'm going with you. Let's get some lunch first though, I'm starved. We need to keep our strength up in case we run into that scumbag on the street."

•••

Deera's parents owned and operated Heavenly Spice Restaurant, a popular eating spot at the entrance to a drab arcade near the central shopping district of Aurora Waters. The majority of orders were take-away at that time of day, and they made themselves comfortable in their regular booth facing the street.

Gemma almost drooled when she inhaled the spicy aromas wafting from the kitchen. Her taste buds knew what was coming and they couldn't wait.

Deera was working and hurried over when she saw them take a seat.

Bec got straight to the point. "I hear you and Lucky have been taking care of our girl."

"We did our best," Deera said. "How are you honey? Did you phone the police?"

"Not yet. Sorry about last night. Bec and I are heading to the police station after lunch."

"There is nothing to be sorry about." Deera's delicate hands twisted and smoothed her apron in turns as she spoke. "I can't imagine what it must have been like for you. Thinking about it gives me the shivers. You will have a better chance of getting there safely if Bec goes with you. I'm worried for you with that maniac on the loose."

After Deera took their orders, the girls barely had time to catch up on the latest gossip before their meals were delivered by unexpected hands.

"We're getting the royal treatment today," Gemma said, "looks like the chefs have brought the kitchen to us."

"Welcome dear friends," Deera's father greeted them with an indulgent smile as he set their orders on the table. "One tandoori chicken for Rebecca, and one vegetable samosas for Gemma."

"Thank you Papa Rishi," Bec replied enthusiastically. "Mama Dar… that jade outfit is divine. How do you manage to stay so glamorous working over a hot stove all day?"

"Thank you Rebecca, you are always very kind." Darshana's brow furrowed as she fixed troubled eyes on Gemma. "My dear girl, Deera informed us of this terrible thing. Why did you not see that crazy person before he accosted you?"

Gemma had already guessed the reason for the couple's rare personal attendance in the dining area. "It's hard to explain. It was after one of Mum's parties, and I was exhausted. Nothing like that has ever happened to me before."

"You must learn to rely on your inner spirit, young one. Let her be your guide. Trust your connection to the supreme soul. Your spirit will protect you."

Darshana had been a big believer in the power of Gemma's inner spirit ever since she had helped to recover her missing necklace. The solid gold chain and emerald pendant was worth a fortune, and its safe return was the main reason for the generous discount the girls always received on their meals.

"The things I see and hear can be pretty vague," she said, trying to justify her slow reactions, "sometimes I need time to interpret them. It all happened so fast. I didn't understand what was going on… and he came at me from behind."

Darshana nodded as if her explanation made perfect sense.

"Next time you get that vague feeling," Bec said, "run away like a frill-necked lizard and figure out what it means later." Her approach was always practical. "Then again… maybe not. You'd only end up running around in circles all day. If in doubt, ask yourself what Daisy would do."

Gemma pretended to shoot Bec with a bow and arrow. "With any luck, there won't be a next time. But I'll try to remember."

"Who is this Daisy, and why would you do as she does?" Rishi scratched his bald head.

"Daisy is a girl we used to hang out with at school," Bec explained. "She was infatuated with a world-famous Aussie adventurer who devoted his life to protecting the environment. When he died in a tragic accident, she was shattered. She was so devastated after hearing the news, her parents arranged an extended camping holiday to help her get over it. Shy, skinny little Daisy was a completely different person by the next time we saw her."

"This Daisy became an adventurer also?"

"More like an adrenaline junkie. She used to tell us stories about mountain climbing and skydiving and other risky stuff she did on weekends. She was into competitive sports like archery too. We haven't seen her since high school, but whenever one of us gets into trouble, we kind of channel her moxie, if you get what I mean."

"And has this strategy ever proven helpful?"

"It's hard to explain," Gemma said. "It sort of takes you out of your own head for a while, which helps sometimes. But it's really only an in-joke between the two of us."

Darshana didn't look convinced. "That is all very well, but you must be more vigilant. This circumstance is not a joke. We have instructed Lucky to keep his eyes on you. He will not allow anything to happen to you."

"You must be cautious—not adventurous," Rishi advised. "This crazy Daisy is not the right role model for you. Sometimes it is more effective to be wary of perilous situations. Your gift is both sacred and highly valuable, you must allow it to guide you *away* from danger. Lucky will help also."

"Thank you so much. I'm grateful for all your advice. I'm sure everything will be fine," Gemma said.

It was a pity she doubted her own assurances. She appreciated their confidence in their son-in-law, but Lucky was a security guard, not a bodyguard. He couldn't be everywhere at once.

CHAPTER FIVE

"Well, how did it go? Can we leave now?" Bec asked when Gemma returned to the waiting area of the police station after making her statement.

"They want me to hang around in case someone needs to speak to me again. I don't know what I was so worried about."

"Do they know who the rodent is? Has anyone else reported him?"

"I didn't ask, and the constable who took my statement didn't volunteer any information. I got the impression he was in a hurry to get it done, so I didn't push it."

Bec wasn't the type of person to sit around doing nothing, and the novelty of their surroundings soon wore off. "What the ho-hum is taking so long?" she grumbled after they were left to loiter for another thirty minutes in the dingy waiting area.

"You go. I'll be OK. It's not as bad as I thought it would be."

"Are you sure? I said I would back you."

"It shouldn't be much longer, and you need to get ready for work." She felt confident the hardest part was over.

Bec rushed off to catch the bus, and not long afterwards, the constable she had spoken to earlier came to collect her. She assumed he would ask her to clarify some details, after which she would be free to go. Instead, he ushered her into a spartan room and shut the door behind her.

Next time the door opened, a snow-capped mountain wearing a charcoal suit and tie walked through it. "Thank you for waiting Ms. Glass. I'm Detective Sergeant Alex Vannen from Aurora Waters CIB. Please take a seat."

She slipped into the closest of two chairs arranged on opposite sides of a rectangular table.

"I thought I would be talking to Constable What's-his-name again."

"There are some irregularities with your statement that I'd like to clarify before you go, if you don't mind."

"Irregularities... really?" The word shattered her composure into a thousand pieces, propelling her overactive imagination in multiple directions at once.

It eventually settled on a particular intrusive image that refused to be shoved aside. The lofty detective reminded her of a Viking character she had seen in a movie once, (only without the long hair, or the beard, or the horned hat). As he lowered his towering frame into the chair opposite her, she studied him surreptitiously from across the table.

"Do you have any objections to our interview being recorded Ms. Glass?"

His polite formality made her nervous. Unsure whether to comply, she stared at the camera as if she would find the answer there.

"It's standard procedure in a complaint of this type."

"Oh, really? I guess that's OK then. Do I need a lawyer or anything?"

"Did you wish to request legal representation for the purpose of this interview?" A dart of suspicion flew through the air between them.

"No. I was just asking." Now she came to think of it, she wasn't sure. Did she need a lawyer? Where did you get a lawyer at short notice?

When he began his spiel, her mind wandered. She was still weighing the advantages and disadvantages of contacting a lawyer, when he asked her to state her name, address, and date of birth for the record. Something felt off, and with doubt came anxiety. She wished she hadn't agreed to the interview after all.

"I'm required to ask if you came here today of your own free will Ms. Glass? Ms. Glass, can you hear me?"

"Oh, sorry. What did you say?"

He repeated the question with the emphasis of a frustrated adult speaking to a child. "Did you... come here today... of your own free will?"

"If you don't count being forced by my friends." A nervous laugh escaped before she could stop it. "Only kidding."

"Please restrict your answers to yes or no when appropriate."

"I only meant that I felt pressured by my friends to report what happened, but I *did* come here voluntarily."

"And has any threat or promise been used to get you to take part in this interview?"

"You said it was standard procedure, so I'll take your word for it. I mean—my answer is *no*—no threats or promises."

"Do you understand that you are not under arrest?"

"Thanks for the clarification. Yes, I understand."

"Do you understand that you are free to leave at any time unless you are arrested?"

"Good to know, yes. Hang on, what do you mean unless I'm arrested?" *That couldn't be right, why would they arrest her?*

"All part of the standard interview procedure. I assure you it will be quite painless." He glanced down at some typewritten notes. "Please describe the alleged incident again for the record, from the beginning. Try not to leave anything out."

It was a challenge to meet his arctic eyes. His hard stare and condescending tone rattled her. *What did he mean by 'alleged incident'?* She wanted to wipe away the beads of perspiration that had formed around her hairline, but she resisted the urge, and hoped he wouldn't notice.

"As I said in my statement, the attack happened on my way home from my parents' house at Larimar yesterday afternoon. I stopped at Bernie's Supermarket for some bread and milk and a frozen meal for dinner."

"For the record, that's Bernie's Bargain Food Mart on Arbor Road?" A shallow dent appeared on one side of his grim face and she couldn't tell if the reaction was related to her choice of supermarket, or the frozen dinner. She guessed it was the latter.

"That's the one. I was walking back to my car with the groceries when it happened."

The nausea induced by her attacker's physical proximity was abruptly restored to the forefront of her recent memory, reigniting her revulsion.

Her first instinct was to avoid the uncomfortable sensations. "On a weekday the shops are packed, but on Sunday, Arbor Road is a lot quieter. So, I parked on the side of the street to save time."

"You were walking back to your car…," he prompted.

"Right. Sorry. I didn't know we were on a time limit. I was giving context."

"Take your time. What happened next?"

"A man grabbed me from behind. He held his hand over my mouth and dragged me backwards." A tremor worked its way into her voice as she relived each horrific moment. No matter how hard she had scrubbed at the places he had touched her, the vile smell of him still clung to her. "I dropped the groceries and tried to pull away, but he was too strong. He said not to struggle, or he would break my neck." She clenched her fists to stop her hands from shaking.

"Did you see his face?"

"No."

"Was there anything familiar about his voice?"

"No."

"What happened next?" He made a brief note in the margins of what she assumed was a copy of her statement.

"A group of Japanese schoolboys jumped off a bus down the road and headed towards the shops."

"How did you know they were Japanese students?"

"They were all wearing the same polo shirt with the words Osaka High School on the front." The scene flashed in front of her eyes and she shivered. "They yelled at the guy and waved their arms… and while he was distracted, I kicked him. When he loosened his grip, I made a run for it."

"Why didn't you alert the police immediately?"

"I was confused. I thought it must be a mistake. I couldn't believe someone was trying to kidnap me."

"You thought it was a kidnapping? Not a robbery… or a sexual assault? Why?"

Wondering what she had gotten herself into, she studied his glacial features for a hint of what he was thinking.

"I don't know why I thought I was being kidnapped. It was a gut feeling." She didn't want to explain exactly how reliable her gut was. "I don't understand any of it."

If she hadn't done anything wrong, why did she feel so guilty? It was *his* fault. He was intimidating her with his penetrating eyes and his politeness. She tried to convince herself that it didn't matter if he believed her or not.

"Now you've had time to think about it, why do you believe someone would want to kidnap you?"

"I have no idea. Maybe he thought I was someone else. Whatever the reason, I don't want it to happen again."

"What prompted you to finally take the step of making an official report? You mentioned threats by your friends."

"That's part of it. They're worried about me. And I don't like the idea that he might do the same thing to someone else. I delayed because I needed time to clear my head and think things through. I didn't want to put myself through something like this if I didn't have to."

"I'm only trying to establish the facts Ms. Glass. No need for alarm if you're telling the truth."

"Why wouldn't I be telling the truth? I didn't do anything wrong."

"Was there anything about this person which would suggest he's known to you?"

"No." She thought about the possibility that she knew him. "But then I didn't see his face, so I can't say for sure."

"What do you do for a living Ms. Glass? The statement lists your occupation as self-employed. What exactly do you do?"

The sudden change of topic took her by surprise. "Oh... uh... I have an online business. And would you mind calling me Gemma? Calling me Ms. Glass all the time puts me off." Hearing her name repeated so formally every time he asked her a question was unsettling, not to mention irritating.

"Whatever you prefer. What type of business?"

She cleared her throat, stalling for time while she tried to think of the least suspicious way to explain her occupation. "I help people find things they've lost."

"I see. Are you a licensed private investigator?"

She wondered whether he suspected her of something disreputable, or if he was just getting his kicks by messing with her head. His blank expression gave nothing away, and her rattled brain imagined him holding his Viking shield, with sword at the ready.

"Ms. Glass… Gemma. I asked if you are a licensed private investigator."

"I didn't know I had to be." She mentally pushed aside the thought of him poking her with his sword. "I don't actually investigate much. All I do is tell people where to look. I sometimes work for a licensed private investigator. At least I assume he's licensed."

"Who do you work for?"

"Harvey Bugg, from Lightning Bugg Investigation Agency. Do you know him?"

"I know *of* him. You were telling me about your online work?"

"It's hard to explain. Potential clients email me with a description of their missing property and I… look into it. If I discover anything helpful, they pay a small fee and I pass on the information to them." She tried to gauge his reaction.

"I see." His blank expression suggested he didn't see at all. "People pay you to tell them where to find their missing property… and you work out what happened to it by virtue of the description they provide. Is that what you said? Did I understand you correctly?"

She thought she had better elaborate before she was arrested for fraud and dragged off to a cell. "You could say I have psychic abilities. It's a type of remote viewing. You've heard of psychics haven't you?"

"That explains a lot."

If suspicion was a lightning bolt, she would have been struck dead.

She tried to describe her business model in a way that he would understand. "I provide information on my website about the types of things I can find, like valuable items or documents, that sort of stuff. I don't offer guarantees. But considering some people spend their hard-earned money to find out who the love of their life will be, I hardly think I'm overcharging. Most of my clients let me know if they were successful. There are plenty of positive testimonials on my website. Here!" She pulled up the page on her phone and shoved it under his nose.

He spent a few minutes skimming through it. "Your clients obviously believe in what you do… Gemma. Or should I call you Gemini from now on?"

"Gemini is my professional name. I thought it would make me sound more like a real psychic."

"Are you saying you're not a *real* psychic?"

"I meant it sounds more like the type of name a psychic would have. Forget it. Next question."

"I suppose if the feedback is genuine, then you must be doing something right."

His grudging acknowledgement prompted her to justify her process further. "I don't charge a fee if I don't have any relevant information to pass on. The method I use doesn't always work. It's as if some things don't want to be found, or they're too far gone."

"Do you ever have requests to find missing persons?"

The question was predictable considering her current location, and it brought to mind the most recent appeal for help she had received.

"There was one last night. I had to explain that I don't offer that particular service." Although the despondent mother's plea had almost ripped her heart out, a particularly disastrous mistake early in her psychic career, had taught her how important it was to remain firm on her policy.

"Have you ever used your abilities in that way?"

"Uh, no."

"Never?"

"No—never. Anyway, why do you want to know what I do for a living? What has it got to do with me being attacked, or abducted, or whatever?"

"It's not a huge leap to suggest your unusual occupation is somehow related to yesterday's attack."

"I guess it could be, but I don't use my real name. How would he have known it was me?"

"It wouldn't be too difficult. These days practically anything, including personal information, is available to anyone who wants it badly enough. Have you always had the ability to find things, or is this a new development?"

"I was diagnosed with blood cancer at the end of my first year of high school. After six months of chemo and radiation I went into remission. Six years later I relapsed. A few more months of chemo… a stem cell transplant… and suddenly I'm seeing things."

Catching herself twisting a strand of hair between her fingers, she dragged her hand away.

"Presumably, you're in remission for a second time?"

"Five years now—fingers crossed." She held up both hands and crossed her fingers as if the ritual would ensure the disease didn't return.

"And there was no indication of anything unusual until after the stem cell treatment?" He tapped his pencil against a point in his notes.

"No. Is it likely that any of this has anything to do with what happened yesterday?"

"It's all quite interesting, but unfortunately you haven't given us much to go on. You didn't see your attacker or get the number plate of his car. Without any other witnesses, there's not a lot we can do from this end."

"What about the Japanese boys?" She felt guilty that she hadn't thought about it at the time.

"Did any of them see anything useful?"

"The boys didn't speak much English. Their teacher did, but I was in such a hurry to get home I didn't get any of their details. Sorry, I wasn't thinking straight. You could probably track them down by checking with local bus companies. Surely there wouldn't be many school groups from Osaka High School seeing the sights around town."

"You may be able to use your ability to track them down for me." Something told her he was making a joke at her expense. "Speaking of which, have you had any psychic revelations about your alleged kidnapper?"

She shook her head. He would be the last person she would want to see again, either in real life or elsewhere.

"That's a shame. If you do see anything, be sure to let me know won't you?" He cracked a smile for the first time, no longer bothering to hide his amusement. "Do you have anything further to add that you feel may be of assistance?"

"I think that covers it." She was relieved the unpleasant experience was finally over and couldn't wait to get out of there.

After formally concluding the official interview, he put her on the spot one last time. "Before you go… Gemma… would you be prepared to provide a demonstration of your ability? It would assist me in better understanding how it actually works."

Was he laughing at her again? Too bad if he was. It could prove interesting to have a peek at Detective Sergeant Vannen's life. If she saw something relevant, it could also prove she wasn't lying.

"I'll give it a try. It's best if I touch you."

His mocking eyes crinkled around the edges. "Do you need bare skin?"

"It could help. Your arm should be fine."

He removed his jacket and rolled up his shirt sleeve. "Be my guest."

From the condition of his arm, it was obvious he wasn't the stereotypical police officer who lived on burgers and donuts. Despite his painful personality, it was almost impossible not to be curious about the rest of the body beneath that charcoal suit. "Are you sure you're a detective? You're younger than most of the ones I've ever seen."

"Have you been interviewed by many detectives?"

"You're the first. But I've seen a few on TV."

This time a muscle at the corner of his mouth twitched. "Then that explains it. I assure you that notwithstanding what you have seen on television, I am a detective sergeant. Would you like to see my badge?"

Another mental picture of him thrusting his Viking shield at her, threatened to wreak havoc with her concentration. "I'm good, thanks. Maybe next time."

Resting her hand lightly on his prominent bicep, she closed her eyes and conjured his stern Nordic features.

In her mind's eye, the lingering impression of his compelling face was joined by those of an attractive woman and small child. The three were posed in the style of a family portrait, with the little girl sharing a loving embrace between the two adults.

For a moment, Gemma was vaguely envious of the aura of genuine happiness that surrounded the idyllic scene; until in a shocking development, the figure of the woman disintegrated, and her ashes were dispersed into the ether as if blown away by some monstrous and unforeseen wind.

The distraught faces of the man and child sent a shockwave of empathy through her, and with the impact of witnessing such a devastating spectacle, the vision faded.

"Well?" His eyes drilled into hers, as if he would be able to see what she had seen if he peered closely enough.

"Nothing—there was nothing there."

Her mind was still struggling to process the revelation. Was it an event that had already occurred or was it a prediction of something that would take place in the future?

"Then I'll be in contact if any further information comes to light about your alleged assailant. Please make yourself available in case we need to question you further."

"But you know everything. There's nothing else to tell."

"You never know what you might remember after the shock wears off. It must have been a distressing ordeal for you. I'll give you my direct phone number in case you think of anything. If you see this man again, either physically or in spirit form, please call me immediately." The trace of a smirk twisted his attempt at a friendly smile.

"Cross my heart, if I see him again you'll be the first to know." She was glad the inquisition was finally over. At least her friends would be happy, she thought, tucking his card inside her wallet.

As she left the building, she felt the urge to look behind, and turned to see him speaking to a plain-clothed amazon at the front desk. Being interrogated by a Viking conqueror had proved to be an unexpectedly annoying experience and she decided she could quite happily forego any further interactions with the police.

•••

"Well Rae, what did you think?" Alex asked his partner as they watched Gemma leave the building. "Was she telling the truth?"

"It's hard to judge through the monitor. She's a strange one, that's for sure. She comes across as a bit of a mix—flaky with a side of kooky. Doesn't strike me as the criminal type though. She tried to hide it, but she was as jumpy as a cat in a kennel. She didn't stop playing with her hair the whole time she was in there. What's that about? Nervous tic?"

Alex smiled at Rae's unconventional character assessment. "Her serious health issues at a young age may have something to do with it, or she might just be the neurotic type. It could also potentially explain why she was so reluctant to report the incident. I believe she's tougher than her body language indicates."

"What was that touchy-feely thing about? You want to get your fortune read? You should have let me know. I could have booked you a session with my Aunt Maisy, she reads a mean tea leaf." Rae barked out a laugh.

"I'm not sure why I encouraged her. I wanted to get more of an idea of how she operates. It could assist with the investigation."

"It's a scam. No big eye-opener there. She certainly didn't have any juicy headlines about you. Nothing at all, in fact. You would think she would have brought out one of those old tried and true, one-size-fits-all, psychic standbys. I see wonderful things in your future… you will crack a major case and earn a big promotion… blah blah blah." Rae did her best impression of a fortune-teller staring hypnotically into a crystal ball.

"You're right. She was surprisingly reluctant to demonstrate the validity of her clairvoyant skills. She may have needed more time to prepare. There would have been scarce opportunity for her to research beforehand. Or she may have been intimidated by her surroundings. Whatever the reason, I have no doubt we need to keep a close eye on the problematic Ms. Gemini. I suspect there is more to her than the interview revealed, and I'm not only referring to her so-called ability. She remains a person of interest as far as the investigation goes."

CHAPTER SIX

Palm Gardens Lifestyle Village was nestled in the verdant valley suburb of Petalmere, roughly a twenty-minute drive southwest of central Aurora Waters.

Her grandmother lived in Bamboo Lodge; one of three wings of serviced units housed in the main building. A high care facility and independent living units made up the balance of the complex, while common amenities attached to each structure, added to a maze-like layout that appeared to be specifically designed to confuse the directionally challenged.

Gemma found her grandmother taking an exercise class in the activities room, where a small band of residents were following the leader with varying degrees of success. Nan was one of the few participants moving her arms and legs in time with the music.

The Palm Gardens Lifestyle Coordinator flitted up beside her as she watched the action from the back of the room. "Your grandmother is very sociable and fit for her age. It's so easy to keep her entertained… unlike some of the other ladies and gentlemen. You should be enormously proud of her."

The lifestyle coordinator's role was to employ all available resources to keep the residents happy, healthy and busily engaged in village life. Rose Honeycomb was the diligent worker bee of the hive, humming with energy and continuously buzzing from one activity to the next. It wasn't necessary to contribute anything more than a nod or murmur of agreement during conversation with her.

"A number of church groups offer their services to our residents, and your grandmother attends every one of their functions," she confided. "If all my charges were like her, it would make my job so much easier." The hint of a wistful sigh followed the remark. "Mrs. Perkins does a wonderful job with the exercise classes. She's such a treasure. I don't know what we would do without her. It looks like they're finishing up. I should move along—lots to do. It's been lovely chatting with you Gemma. Enjoy your visit dear." A distracted expression streaked across her angular face before she flapped a bony hand and dashed away.

At the completion of the activity, most of the group members wandered off to the next event on their social calendars for the day, except for one woman, who collapsed into a lounge chair, puffing, and panting to catch her breath.

In contrast, Nan had barely raised a sweat, remaining impeccable in her blue jersey tracksuit.

"You were quick. I must have caught you at exactly the right time. I won't hug you because I'm smelly. How are you sweetie?" She patted Gemma on the cheek, then took both hands and held her at arm's length. "You look different. You're paler than usual, have you been to see Dr. Hudson?"

"I'm good Nan. I've been to lunch with Bec. How are you feeling? You sounded upset on the phone."

"Come back to my unit while I freshen up. I'll make us a cup of tea and we'll talk."

Nanna Glass had moved a few precious keepsakes with her to Palm Gardens after her husband died, and while she changed out of her exercise clothes, Gemma waited in the living area of her simple unit, surrounded by cherished family furniture and memorabilia.

On the sideboard was a framed snapshot of her grandfather, happily dozing in his battered rocking chair, with her baby-self sound asleep in his arms.

Nan emerged from her bedroom wearing a fresh lilac lounge suit. "I almost feel like he's still with us sometimes," she said when she saw Gemma looking at the photo. As they settled into the well-worn armchairs with their cups of tea, her face wilted beneath the strain of whatever was bothering her. "I miss him so much. I could always depend on him in a sticky situation."

"What's wrong Nan?" Gemma hadn't seen her so agitated since the day the family had said their final goodbyes to Pop.

"Something strange has happened and I don't know what to do." Her floral cup wobbled precariously as she set it down on its matching saucer. "You're so clever, just like your grandfather. I know you'll be able to help."

Gemma's sixth sense sounded an alarm. "I'll do my best. What happened?"

"I've made a new friend named Frank Malloy." The words tumbled into an expectant void.

Nothing alarming about that, she thought. "That's a good thing, isn't it? He hasn't made a move on you, has he?"

"Don't be silly. It's nothing like that. We play cards together. Your grandfather and I played euchre for years, and a group of us started a competition here in the village. We call it the World Championship Euchre Tournament. It's just a bit of fun. Frank and I always play as a team. We're the current world champions." The hint of a smile threatened to make an appearance before disappearing back into the creases of her worried frown.

"That's one way to become world champions I suppose," Gemma mused. "Has Frank been off his game lately?"

"He hasn't been playing at all, that's the problem. He's missing."

"What do you mean by missing? Start at the beginning."

"I can't believe he would take off without saying anything to anyone… without saying anything to me. He would never forfeit a game. The title meant too much to him."

"Does he carry a phone?"

"I've left messages. I've practically begged him to get in touch, but he hasn't replied."

"Does anyone else know about this?"

"I went to the manager. She was no help. All she would say was that he was having a short holiday with relatives, and that she was sure he would be back when he was ready."

"There you are then. The manager wouldn't have any reason to lie, would she?"

"It doesn't make sense. Frank told me that he never has anything to do with his family. 'They're a pack of money-grubbing lowlifes.' They were his exact words."

"Have you checked with his other friends in the village?" The siren wailing inside Gemma's head was growing increasingly louder.

"No one remembers seeing him since last Friday, not that that means anything. Some of them can't even remember what they had for breakfast half the time. The only other person who might know something is one of the gardeners. Frank spends a lot of time in the gardens, especially when Bill is working. He's working today, but I haven't had a chance to speak with him yet."

"I'm sorry your friend wasn't here for your card game. Try not to let it get you down. Who knows, he could be back any minute."

"Please sweetie, you know I wouldn't ask if it wasn't urgent. Frank might be in trouble and I would never forgive myself if anything happened to him. If you don't see anything suspicious, I promise I won't bother you again. Your grandfather would want you to help your poor old Nanna."

Nan didn't understand the potential consequences of what she was asking, but it was impossible to refuse her when she used Pop's memory as leverage.

"All right, but don't tell anyone I did this for you. Do you have a photo?" She hoped that neither of them would end up regretting it.

"This one was taken right after the presentation of the championship trophy." It was a snapshot of Nan and an elderly gentleman with receding hair and a round belly. The triumphant couple wore smiles almost as wide as the man's middle.

"Are you sure it wasn't the lottery you two won?"

"Frank was so excited. He kept talking about how the euchre tournament was the most fun he'd had in years. He boasted to everyone how we were undefeated. He even suggested inviting other retirement homes to join the competition." Her words were upbeat, but her voice pleaded for reassurance.

"I'm sure he's fine. He may be back already, and you don't even know it." Gemma hugged her grandmother before turning her attention to the photograph.

She closed her eyes, only to find her mind was awash with dizzying darkness. Frank's face had disappeared, and instinctively, she knew something was wrong. She didn't understand why, but her usual process hadn't worked.

Abandoning the search, she expected to open her eyes to her grandmother's cluttered unit. Instead, she was faced with four bare walls in a cavernous space. The only explanation was that she had bypassed the portal and landed inside the other dimension, and her first thought was that the last time something similar had happened, things hadn't ended well.

A large picture window on one wall overlooked a suburban street, and the familiarity of the surrounding landscape—combined with the lack of furniture in the room—implied the elderly man could be helping a relative move. Encouraged to explore further, she projected her thoughts through an open doorway and sensed the corresponding shift in her astral body.

That's when she spotted Frank, slumped in a chair in the adjoining room. His pallid skin was coated in a waxy sheen and his slack jaw rested open-mouthed on his chest. The jovial face that had so recently beamed with delight at his trophy-winning exploits, had been replaced by a gruesome death mask.

A wave of static blasted through Gemma at the distressing sight, and when her head cleared, she was staring into her grandmother's crystal blue irises. Confused and slightly disoriented, she tried to avoid her probing gaze.

"What's wrong sweetie? Your eyes went blank for a few minutes, and now you're as white as a sheet. What happened?"

She did her best to disguise the impact of what she'd seen. "I think Frank is staying at a house in the local area."

"Thank heavens. Then it was all for nothing. How did he seem?"

"He was sitting around… not up to much. It's weird he hasn't called you. How about I find the gardener and see if he's heard anything?" She was eager to get out from under her grandmother's savvy scrutiny.

Before she got the chance to make her exit, there was a knock at the door.

"That will be Morgan, probably here to collect the dirty linen."

Morgan Payne was in Gemma's grade in high school. Her official title was lifestyle assistant, but her job description covered everything from serving meals to scrubbing bathrooms. Whenever they ran into each other, she demonstrated the same unpleasant personality traits that had been her trademark for as long as Gemma had known her.

Morgan didn't bother to knock twice, barging into the room before Nan could answer the door. "Gloria, you're home. I knew you wouldn't mind if I let myself in." Heavy lipliner accentuated the fleshy volume that overwhelmed the lower half of her face. "You have a visitor. Oh wait, it's only Gemma. I thought it was somebody interesting for a minute."

"I'm thrilled to see you too Morgan. What's new?"

"Wouldn't you like to know. I'll let you in on a little secret. It won't be long before I say goodbye to all the senile geriatrics in this dreary dump." She directed a sickly-sweet smirk at Nan. "Present company excepted, naturally."

Gemma was used to ignoring Morgan's sarcastic comments but was curious about why she would wear a full face of makeup to clean toilets. "Do you have a hot date after work, or are you trying to impress the male residents?"

"I have a hectic social life, unlike some people."

Morgan was always dating *someone*. "Nan was telling me she hasn't seen her friend Frank around lately. She's been trying to contact him, but he's not returning her calls. You wouldn't happen to have any inside info—would you?"

"How should I know where the old codger is? As if I would care. One less grumpy old fart for me to clean up after. Pity they all didn't take more holidays. It would reduce my workload."

"I swear they could launch a space probe inside that blood sucker's brain and not find signs of intelligent life," Nan said after she left.

It was common knowledge Morgan hated her job, and her questionable conduct was always a hot topic of conversation around the village. Not only did she take every opportunity to shirk her duties, some of the residents had also caught her going through their personal belongings. A delegation had complained to management, but she had denied everything. Excuses were made and nothing was done.

If she had any information about Frank, it was clear she wasn't prepared to share it.

After exchanging insults with her disagreeable school nemesis, Gemma was in even more need of fresh air. She wasn't sure what she would achieve by questioning Bill, but it made her feel as though she was doing something to help. Promising to talk to the gardener, she kissed her grandmother goodbye and headed outside to find him.

During her tour of the grounds, there were no signs of any underlying tension or hostility, and the staff members she observed along the way appeared respectful and conscientious, encouraging her to hope that Morgan was a unique case. The greatest mystery involving Palm Gardens before Frank's disappearance, was why Morgan hadn't been sacked ages ago.

In the lush gardens surrounding the accommodation areas, a wide variety of trees and palms provided a billowy canopy of dappled shade. Tropical flowers bloomed between golden canes and foxtail palms with broad, feathery fronds protected those enjoying the outdoor amenities from the burning rays of the sun.

Reflecting the general air of contentment, a black and white butterfly fluttered above her head for a few moments, before settling on a leafy shrub nearby. Deep in thought as she watched it draw nectar from a bright pink bud, she failed to notice a camouflaged figure kneeling alongside the path.

"You better watch where you're going, or you'll end up face down in the dirt."

"Sorry. I didn't see you. Your name is Bill, isn't it?" She had never spoken to the gardener before and didn't want to make him suspicious about her motives.

"Hmm."

"I'm Gemma. Gloria from Bamboo Lodge is my grandmother. I've been admiring your lovely garden."

"Hmm."

"Nan said that her friend, Frank, likes to hang out in the garden… and that he's a friend of yours as well."

"I know Frank."

Gemma had seen Bill working around the village plenty of times but hadn't paid a lot of attention to him before. She was curious whether he was rude to everyone, or if she was getting special treatment. He continued to pull weeds as they spoke, or as she asked questions and he grudgingly replied.

"Nan was disappointed when Frank missed their card game this morning. Have you heard anything from him recently?"

He glared up at her from beneath his wide brimmed hat. "I haven't seen him since last Friday. He was chirpy enough then. Most likely he's busy going about his life and minding his own bees wax."

The irritable responses weren't encouraging, but she gave it one last shot. "Nan will be glad to hear that. Did he happen to mention that he intended to visit his family over the weekend?"

The gardener's hooded eyes registered a hint of surprise. "How Frank spends his weekends is his business. I best be going now. I have a lot of work to do." He picked up his tools and the bucket of weeds and walked away without answering her question.

Investigating missing persons was harder than it sounded. Disappointed, but not discouraged, she considered her next move. Someone must know something. Nan had already spoken to the manager and Frank's other friends. There was only one other person she could think of who might be helpful, and she hiked back to the main building to find Rose.

The industrious lifestyle coordinator was setting up a game of bingo in the activities room. "You're still here, dear? Is anything wrong?"

"I was on my way to the manager's office. Nan is worried about her friend Frank, so I told her I would try to find out when he'll be back. She's been asking around, but she said no one has heard anything. If Ms. Meyer was able to get a message to him for her, it would put her mind at ease."

"I wish I had known your grandmother was concerned. I could have reassured her. Residents often go to stay with family and friends. It isn't unusual by any means. We need to be mindful of Mr. Malloy's privacy. If he isn't responding to phone calls, he must have his reasons. Don't worry, I'll make sure your grandmother is so busy she won't have time to fret."

Gemma had exhausted all her ideas. Nobody except Nan seemed to care about where Frank had gone. There was nothing else she could do, so she made her way towards the front entrance, more confused than ever.

"Psst! Hey girlie, over here." The wiry senior citizen the other residents called The Cherry Man, was perched on a wooden bench in a shady spot outside the main entrance. He wore the shirt with the cherries on it that prompted his nickname.

"I'm getting out of this place," he mumbled.

"Are you talking to me?" She checked to make sure they were alone.

"It's not safe here. Get out while you can."

"Why do you say that? What do you mean 'it's not safe'?"

"My nephew is on his way. He'll be here soon to pick me up. I told him what they're up to, and he's coming to get me."

"What are they up to? Who are they? Is someone here up to something?" The Cherry Man wasn't exactly the most reliable source, but after what she had seen, she had to be sure.

"My nephew is a famous Hollywood actor. I explained what's going on here—about the experiments—and he's coming to get me. He'll be here any minute."

One of the village nurses strode through the front entrance doors. "There you are Stewart. I should have known you'd be here. It's time for your medication. You'd better come with me."

"He says his nephew is coming to pick him up."

"That's right. A couple of times a week we find him out here waiting for his nephew. Poor man, he suffers from delusions. He's harmless, but it doesn't help that he never gets any visitors. I suppose he explained that his nephew is a famous Hollywood actor?"

"Among other things. I hope he'll be OK."

"He'll settle down once he has his medication."

CHAPTER SEVEN

With her involvement in Frank's disappearance, Gemma's life had taken on an even more surreal quality than usual. The impulse to comfort her grandmother had presented her with an impossible dilemma, and because she wasn't sure if she could handle it on her own, she was desperate enough to seek parental advice. Her mother's open invitation to dinner was also the easiest way to solve the problem of her empty pantry.

After leaving Palm Gardens, she dropped into her apartment long enough to grab Bones and pack a change of clothes.

"You're going to visit Lucas. You'll like that, won't you Bobo?" she told him as she lugged his hefty travel crate downstairs to the garage. "Please don't make a fuss. We'll be there in no time. I promise."

His pitiful whines started the second she loaded him onto the back seat of her car and continued until she pulled up in front of her parents' house in Larimar.

While juggling the weight of both her physical and mental burdens up the front path, she was spooked by a rustling sound in the bushes. Her nerves were already frazzled by the grating din of her anxious ragdoll's incessant complaints, and with heart racing, she whirled around to identify the source.

There was no one there, and when Bones broke the tension by meowing his disapproval, she rushed inside, locking the door behind her.

"What's wrong boy? Is the wicked witch scaring you?" Lucas was waiting for them in the hall. Ignoring Gemma, he made a beeline for the crate and scooped the heavy cat into his skinny arms.

"If I'm the wicked witch, then you're the flying monkey," she said to herself as he clumped off with Bones.

"Lucas!" she called after him.

"What?"

"Were you spying on me as I walked up the path?"

"So what? I heard a car drive up and I was working on my surveillance techniques. What of it? I wanted to know if you brought Bones with you."

"Did you see anyone out the front of the house? Or in the yard? Any strangers hanging around?"

"There *was* someone."

"What were they doing?" The sick feeling that had started outside the front door, shot to her chest in palpitating waves.

"You said someone strange?"

"Come on, spit it out. Put those spying eyes to good use for a change." If she passed on the information to Detective Vannen it might make up for some of her previous failures.

"I saw *you*. You're the only *strange* one that's been around here today—except for Dad." He whooped at his own comic brilliance as he walked away, and Gemma groaned under her breath. If she couldn't see that coming, what hope did she have?

Her father was in the TV room, and only tore his eyes away from the racing channel long enough to mumble a greeting as she passed.

Her mother was in the kitchen, up to her elbows in dinner preparation, wooden spoon in one diminutive hand and crystal champagne flute in the other. "What did you get up to today, my darling? There's an open bottle if you want some."

A glop of spaghetti sauce catapulted from the spoon and splattered on the refrigerator door as she gestured towards the location of the bottle. Alcohol and cooking could be a messy and sometimes dangerous combination for Kristin Glass. She planted a candy pink kiss on Gemma's cheek before taking another sip of bubbly.

"You've got dark circles under your eyes. Have you been working for that horrible Harvey Grubb character again?"

"It's Harvey Bugg—not Grubb. At least since I've been working for him, I'm finally managing to save a little money. Who knows, I might even be able to replace Pop's old car one day."

"Whatever his name is, his googly eyes give me the creeps. You were lucky to get that car. It's been very reliable, considering how long it's been in the family. Although I suppose it will give up the ghost one day."

Gemma flinched. "I know Harvey's not exactly the most attractive person in the world, but he pays well."

"It's not only that—the work could be dangerous. Private investigation agencies come into contact with a lot of shady characters."

"I need the agency money to pay the bills. It's not like I can eat the lingerie you give me." They looked at each other. "Then again, I suppose I *could* eat some of it. I doubt if it would have much nutritional value though."

Her mother's flushed face cracked a slightly boozy grin. "If it's the extra money you're after, you could always host your own parties. I could give you some leads."

"You and Dad have been helping me out long enough. I want to try things my way." After her mother's comments about the possible dangers involved in working for Harvey, she concluded it wasn't the right time to mention that she had been attacked. "I went to see Nanna Glass this afternoon. Have you spoken to her recently?"

"Not lately. Why?"

"She thinks something has happened to her friend, a man by the name of Frank Malloy. She wanted me to look for him."

"That must have been awkward."

"I wasn't happy about it, but I couldn't say no to Nan."

Her father joined them at the breakfast bar. It was all sports and world news until something got his attention, and usually that *something* meant bad news for her or Lucas. "What's going on? What's this Malloy character got to do with your grandmother?"

"He's her euchre partner. Nan was upset because he missed their card game this morning."

"Don't waste your time worrying about some stranger you don't even know. Concentrate on your own problems. Mum should learn to stop poking her nose into other people's business."

"Let's have a few drinks and a lovely dinner and relax," her mother suggested. "I'm sure this Frank Malloy will show up safe and sound, and everyone will have gone to a lot of bother for nothing."

If only it was that easy. Gemma's conscience wouldn't let it rest. How could she stay out of it when she was suspicious about Frank's fate? At least when he was finally found, Nan's nose-poking would be justified, and her mother and father would be forewarned about her involvement.

Anticipating the need for a bubbly sedative or two, she was prepared to stay the night in her old bedroom. Her parents hadn't changed anything since she had moved out, and once she was comfortably entrenched among her adolescent possessions, she thought about her next move.

When Nan asked her to locate her missing friend, she unwittingly transferred the burden of his welfare, and she was highly motivated to shift that burden to more capable shoulders. She was already plagued by guilt after what she had seen and didn't want the responsibility of explaining Frank's probable demise. That was a job for someone with more authority, or at the very least, more experience in dealing with the discovery of dead bodies.

She wondered how Detective Vannen would react if she passed on her doubts about Frank. Would he take it seriously, given who the information was coming from? What was the worst thing that could happen? He was already dubious about the way she earned a living, and she had a fair idea he thought she was touched in the head.

Her eyes gravitated towards some school photos mounted on the bedroom wall, and she recalled her earlier conversation with Bec. Daisy wouldn't let someone else's opinion stop her from doing anything.

She picked up her phone.

"Detective Vannen, this is Gemma Glass. I'm sorry if I'm calling too late." Her voice sounded shaky to her own ears. She had assumed the call would go to voicemail.

"Too late for *what* Ms. Glass?"

"I meant late at night. Never mind. This is going to sound mad, but I think I've seen a dead body." The silence was ominous. "Are you there?"

She pictured him on another phone line, assembling a SWAT team to arrest her.

"Are you certain this person was deceased?"

Frank's gruesome corpse flashed in front of her eyes. "If he's not dead, then he's in a very bad way and needs serious help."

"Where did you see this allegedly deceased person Ms. Glass?"

She could tell he was annoyed and almost regretted her decision to call him. But she had already let the cat out of the bag, so she had to see it through. "Uh… you know, the place I sometimes see things." She couldn't quite manage to put it into words over the phone.

"Are you telling me you saw this person in a vision?"

"It's kind of a long story. My grandmother asked me to check on a friend of hers. They both live at Palm Gardens Lifestyle Village. She hasn't seen him around recently and she's worried about him. So, I looked… and I found him. Now I don't know what to do."

"I thought you said you never used your ability to find missing persons?"

"Did I? I meant hardly ever… and only under *really* special circumstances… and only if I think there's no *possible* way to avoid it." She imagined him pulling his hair out, one frosty icicle at a time.

"All right, I get the point. What time did you have this revelation?"

"This afternoon."

"And you're only reporting this now?"

"I was confused. I talked to some of the staff, and they said he was visiting relatives. It's possible I'm wrong, but I can't help feeling that I'm not. I didn't know what else to do under the circumstances, especially since I know you already think I've got a screw loose."

"You know that—do you? And what gave you that impression?"

"The expression you get on your face when I talk about seeing things… and the tone of your voice. I'm not judging you. I have trouble believing it myself most of the time."

"I'm prepared to give you the benefit of the doubt on this occasion. What do you need from me?"

"To find out what happened to my grandmother's friend. His name is Frank Malloy. I thought that was your job."

"Do you have any idea where this Frank Malloy's corpse is currently located?"

"The street name is Wattle something. I got the impression it's somewhere local, but I'm not sure of that either. I don't know the house number or which suburb it's in, but I think the house was vacant. What are you going to do now?"

"You haven't given me a lot to go on, as usual. I'll check into it and let you know if anything turns up. What about your assailant? Have you had any further encounters?"

"Nothing so far. I promise you'll be the first to know."

"Be aware that it would be in your best interests to notify the authorities immediately next time you see something that has legal implications. Not only your psychic abilities are in question."

"Sure, sorry about that." *Next time I see a dead body, I'll ring you straight away,* she added under her breath.

"I'll be in touch." He ended the conversation as abruptly as he had answered the phone.

Gemma tried to convince herself that she had fulfilled all of her moral obligations. Overall, the conversation with Detective Vannen had exceeded her expectations. Her burden of guilt had been lifted considerably, knowing responsibility now rested squarely on particularly broad shoulders. She supposed it was his job to be suspicious of everyone, but she was puzzled about exactly what he meant when he said it wasn't *only* her psychic abilities in question.

•••

Whenever she fed Bones anything other than his preferred brand of cat food, his sensitive stomach's ultimate rejection typically resulted in putrid piles of cat vomit all over her bedroom carpet. Why throw up on tiles when carpet was so much harder to clean? To keep his tummy happy and her carpet vomit free, (and restock the void inside her kitchen cabinets), a trip to the local supermarket was at the top of her agenda for the day.

Shopping trends had returned to normal since the havoc of the virus had prompted tedious lines of impatient customers to hoard every non-perishable food and disinfectant product in sight. Early mornings at the supermarkets were again relatively crowd-free, as most of the tourists were either at the beach or still sleeping off the previous night's round of clubs and parties.

Following a hasty breakfast with her family, she negotiated the busy morning traffic parade of local tradespeople, office workers, and school run caregivers, to drop Bones off at her apartment. Less than half an hour later, she headed out again to Brollies Supermarket in the adjoining suburb of Crescent Cove, the most convenient source of the Ocean Casserole brand of cat cuisine.

The drama of her last shopping experience had faded after recent events had skyrocketed to the top of her list of scary things, and she was engrossed in reading the fine print on a dolphin-safe label in the pet food aisle, when the shock of a hard body jolting against her, brought her crashing back to reality.

She dived for cover, bracing herself behind her trolley, intending to wield the mobile metal basket to defend herself against the threat.

"I'm so sorry. Are you all right? Did I hurt you? Are you in pain?"

The apologetic culprit wasn't dangerous, it was only a clumsy idiot not watching where he was going.

She glared at the offending klutz from behind the barrier of the trolley, and the repentant face staring back at her, belonged to the only other person besides her ex who had ever captured her romantic interest. It *was* someone dangerous after all. Her thoughts were immediately flooded by memories of the star athlete she had been infatuated with at school.

"No harm done." Her thudding heart threatened to burst through the walls of her chest, and she tried to pretend she was only breathless due to the collision.

His remorseful eyes flashed with recognition. "Gemma? Is that you? Did I hurt you? It's Eli Nite. I went to Shellgarden High School."

Eli had been a member of the football team and had gone out of his way to be kind to her after her diagnosis. He had played a key role in her early teenage years, (if only in her fantasies).

"Eli... no... I mean yes... I didn't... you didn't... I think neck braces are on special this week. What are you doing here?" She couldn't believe he remembered her, or how much she rambled when she was nervous.

"I'm in town on business and forgot to pack a few things. You know how it is. I'm sorry if I hurt you. Instead of a neck brace, would a massage be more beneficial? My treat."

"You didn't really hurt me. Although now that you mention it, a massage would be nice. It was lucky you told me who you were, I was about to ram you with my trolley. You caught me by surprise."

She suddenly regretted her choice of outfit. A boho sundress and a lick of mascara didn't quite measure up to his luxury brand suit.

"I'm glad you're not hurt. Are you sure there's nothing else I can do to make it up to you?"

Aside from his looks and athletic prowess, Eli's kindness was the main reason she had developed a major crush on him at school. She was glad he hadn't changed. "I'm fine, really. How have you been?"

"Life is hectic. I'm sure you can relate."

She would have liked to prolong the moment for old times' sake but rejected the temptation to channel the pathetic lovesick groupie from school days. "Me too. Very busy! I hope you enjoy your stay. It's great to see you again. I should get back to my shopping. I have a starving cat waiting for me at home." *If that didn't scare him off, nothing would.*

"I hate to think your cat would wither away to nothing on my account. We could get together later this evening. Preferably somewhere without fluorescent lights and the risk of being run over by careless brutes." He indicated their current surroundings with a tilt of his stylish head. "I'd like to hear what you've been up to since high school."

His suggestion was unanticipated, considering her loser excuse about her starving cat. She was flattered and wanted to accept his invitation, but ultimately conceded to an overwhelming urge to avoid inevitable disappointment.

"I don't think I can. I've had a lot going on lately and I'm falling behind with work." The lame excuse was all she could think of on the spur of the moment.

"That's a shame. I never made it to any of the school reunions for the same reason. I thought while I was in town, I would try to catch up with a few people from school. I believe some of them still live around Aurora Waters. A little local knowledge could prove useful in tracking them down."

"In that case, how can I refuse?" She couldn't tell which one of them was more surprised at her sudden change of heart. "I'm not sure how much use I'll be with tracking down your friends, but I'll help if I can."

"For a moment I thought you were about to turn me down. I'm glad you reconsidered. I'm staying at the Meridian. I know of an excellent seafood restaurant at Fairhaven Marina. How does that sound?"

"That's Celestial Seafood. It sounds great." She was embarrassed to tell him it was out of her price range.

"I'll make a reservation. Say around seven? Will that be enough time to get up to date with your work and ensure your feline dependent is watered and fed?"

"Perfect. I'll meet you outside the restaurant at seven. Here's my number in case the plan changes."

"Are you sure you wouldn't like me to pick you up? I have a rental."

"My apartment isn't far from the marina. Where you're staying is only a short walk, so you won't really need your car. But thanks for the offer."

Bones appeared as if by magic as soon as she dumped the shopping bags onto her kitchen bench, head-bumping her leg and complaining with a persistent *feed me* meow. If she didn't respond quickly enough, his next move would be to nip the exposed areas of her calf. Then if mild persuasion didn't achieve the desired result, the bites would grow more demanding and consequently more painful. If none of his other tactics worked, he would claw the laminate on the kitchen drawers.

Not wanting to provoke any further pain or damage if she could avoid it, she emptied a can of his beloved Ocean Casserole into a bowl and set it on his feeding mat. Then while he was greedily occupied, snuffling and snorting with insatiable delight, she unpacked the remainder of the groceries and thought about what she should wear to dinner. It had been a while since she had been to a fancy restaurant, and she wondered if she owned anything suitable.

A brief message from Eli confirmed the details of their reservation, and along with the flutter of anticipation that accompanied it, came speculation about what she had gotten herself into.

Her phone sat on the kitchen bench while she worked, and whenever it hovered in the corner of her eye, she was reminded of her promise to update Bec on what had happened at the police station after she left. She would have liked more time to sort through her emotions before opening herself up to another grilling, but she couldn't put it off indefinitely.

"Oh my God, I can't believe you ran into Eli Nite," Bec squealed, after Gemma had filled her in on current events. "What's he doing back in Aurora Waters? Is he living here now?"

"He's here for work. We were standing in the middle of the supermarket, so I was hardly going to ask for his life story. He said he wants to catch up with some old school friends while he's here."

She failed to mention that the only reason she had accepted the dinner invitation, was an unsettling vision she had seen of Eli consorting with Morgan Payne. The last thing she wanted was for Bec to jump to conclusions.

"Why don't you drop into the casino after dinner? I'd be interested to see how he turned out."

"I'll think about it. Let's see how dinner goes first."

"What about this detective who interviewed you yesterday? What's he like? You didn't say much about him."

"I'm not sure what to think about Detective Vannen. He was rude… and unsympathetic. I felt like I was being interrogated. Then when I rang him about Nan's friend, he said I could get into trouble with the police if I didn't keep them informed."

"Sounds like a jerk. What does he look like?"

"I tell you the way he treated me and all you care about are superficial details."

"It's not all I care about, but we can forgive him a little if he's gorgeous."

"We can—can we?" Gemma wasn't so sure about that. "I wouldn't exactly call him gorgeous. He's taller than average, with piercing blue eyes that make me nervous."

"In a sexy way or an irritating way?"

"In an uncomfortable way… like he's suspicious… like he's trying to see inside my head."

"Is he married?"

"How should I know? I was a little busy being unjustifiably probed. It didn't occur to me to ask about his love life."

"Ooh… there's nothing like a bit of double entendre to get the pre-dinner hormones pumping."

"Pity it relates to the wrong individual."

"Somebody's touchy. I think I hit a nerve."

"Let's say he managed to get under my skin. I'm not sure how I feel about him otherwise. He's younger than I thought a detective would be. And easy on the eye, in a brooding, ruthless kind of way. But Eli is good-looking *and* likeable, and he's the one I'm seeing tonight. Forget about Detective Vannen."

"Detective Vannen is a dick and Eli is a babe. Got it. Don't take everything so seriously. I need a coffee fix and you need to find something to wear. Make sure you bring Eli to the casino tonight. I can't wait to see how some of those superficial details have matured."

Amused by Bec's blunt portrayal of the two men, Gemma hung up and turned her attention to the task of inspecting her wardrobe. Whatever Eli's real purpose for asking her out, she wanted him to be glad he did. There could be a reasonable explanation for her vision of him and Morgan. He could have been visiting a relative at Palm Gardens and run into her while he was there. He was being polite, and it only looked as though he was responding to her amorous advances. He was probably secretly repulsed by her pert nose and impertinent boobs.

She decided to work with that scenario for the time being and give him the benefit of the doubt. But deep down she couldn't ignore the possibility that Morgan was up to something, and if that was the case, she was determined to find a way to turn the tables on her.

Deera responded eagerly to her plea for help, arriving promptly with an assortment of makeup kits and hair styling tools in tow.

"You've got a date, how exciting," she gushed as she arranged Gemma's bedroom like a beauty salon. "Where is he taking you?"

"We're meeting at Celestial Seafood at seven. I'm not sure if it's a date or if it's just two people who went to the same high school making plans for a reunion. I can't believe he remembered me."

"Go out and have a little fun for a change," Deera encouraged her. "Make sure you look amazing and then even if he didn't intend it to be a romantic evening, it soon will be."

"I'll try to go with the flow and stop overthinking things. I need one of those head massages they give you after you have your hair washed. It would help me relax." She had been fixated on the idea of a massage ever since Eli had suggested it.

Deera set to work enthusiastically, reminding Gemma of Cinderella's fairy godmother, flitting around the room with her curling wand and working her magic in a hundred different ways. She even added a quick scalp massage. All that remained to complete the look, was to slide into her dress.

"Thank you so much," she said, surprised at her reflection in the bedroom mirror. "Is that really me? My hair looks great. Are you sure it's not over the top?"

Deera stood back to gauge the overall effect of her handiwork. "You should curl your hair more often, it suits you. And that eye palette is inspired. I missed my calling as a personal stylist if I do say so myself. You can never be too ravishing—trust me."

Before returning to her own apartment, she made Gemma promise to send her a selfie once her outfit was complete.

Despite a distinct lack of motivation, Gemma used the rest of the afternoon to catch up on work. After her experience at Wattle Street and the random vision of Eli and Morgan, she couldn't be sure what to expect, so she proceeded with caution. Thankfully, the next few hours turned out to be business as usual, resulting in a number of positive outcomes, without any unpleasant surprises.

Convinced that she had earned enough to pay for Bones' monstrous appetite for another week, she assessed her appearance in the mirror one last time before leaving for the restaurant. Hidden beneath her tight fitting sheath dress was the steamy lingerie she had received for working at Angela's hen's party. She had hoped the lingerie would give her confidence, but that was probably just one of her mother's sales ploys. She wasn't sure that she was appropriately dressed to catch up with a casual acquaintance for dinner and a chat, but there was no time to change.

CHAPTER EIGHT

Eli was waiting for her at the entrance to the restaurant. "Perfect timing. You look sensational." His admiring gaze confirmed that Deera's efforts had been worthwhile. As his lips brushed her cheek, she breathed in the earthy scent of his aftershave, glad when his proximity failed to generate anything more unnerving than a fluttering heartbeat.

Catching her hand, he led her through the indoor dining area towards a spacious deck. "We have a table overlooking the marina, but it can be changed to one inside if you prefer."

The reflection of the vessel lights extended the panorama of the night sky across the water, creating the illusion the deck was floating in space, surrounded by stars.

"Why would we move inside when we can sit out here? No wonder so many high rollers live on their million-dollar yachts… with the Meridian Casino so close, they'd be crazy not to."

A hovering waiter arranged their place settings and filled their water glasses, before leaving them alone to browse the menu.

"I could stare at this view all night," she said, in awe of the dazzling outlook.

"I know exactly what you mean."

Something in his voice made her look at him. "You're not watching the water."

"I don't have to—the lights are reflected in your eyes. The view is even better there."

She questioned the motivation behind the comment, given her suspicions about his association with Morgan. "I bet you tell that to all the girls from school."

"Why would you doubt my sincerity?"

His wounded expression startled her, and she scrambled to explain her reluctance to accept his compliment. "I thought you were flattering me."

"I *was* flattering you, but that doesn't mean it isn't true." His jaw relaxed. "Your eyes are both beautiful and extraordinary… like watching a meadow of fireflies in the moonlight. The moment I saw you this morning, I remembered you. It was a pleasant surprise when you accepted my dinner invitation, especially after literally running into you at the supermarket."

"I guarantee I was more surprised than you were. You could have knocked me over with a trolley."

Her attempt at banter prompted a seductively ingenuous smile from him, prompting a couple of her heartbeats to trip over one another.

"How long have you been back in town?"

"Not long. I flew in on Sunday. How about you? Did you stay in Aurora Waters after you finished school?"

She was disappointed when he didn't volunteer further details about his visit. "I'm not likely to leave," she admitted. His question made her think of Ryan, and she wondered how much Eli knew about her life after school. "I'm happy here. I like living close to the beach and my family. My parents and younger brother live at Larimar, and my grandmother lives at Palm Gardens Lifestyle Village."

The mention of Palm Gardens drew no reaction from him, and before she could explore the topic further, he changed the subject to a discussion of the menu.

The waiter arrived soon afterwards to take their order, and because she intended to pay her own way, she settled for the least expensive menu items she could find for starter and main course.

At the other end of the price spectrum, Eli opted for natural rock oysters and lobster, and chose an expensive bottle of Sauvignon Blanc to accompany their meals. While dismayed at the cost of the wine, she went along with his selection, relying on the alcohol to help loosen his tongue.

"Speaking of Palm Gardens," she said, "someone I know works there. Do you remember Morgan Payne?"

He didn't answer immediately, appearing preoccupied with a speck of dust on his wine glass. "The name rings a bell. Was she the girl who used to star in all the school musicals?"

"No. That's my best friend, Bec. She has the voice of an angel and the temper of a grizzly bear. Morgan wasn't a close friend at school. I run into her occasionally when I visit Nan at the village." It was an understatement, but factual.

"Morgan Payne… now I remember. She was an outgoing girl. Quite a character if memory serves."

Another burst of his electric smile disarmed her, and she felt a touch of heat on the surface of her skin. Flames from the candlelight melted her determination as she was drawn to their reflection in his eyes. She wanted to believe him, and it took all her self-control to maintain her concentration.

The flame flickered, breaking the spell. "Have you been back to Aurora Waters for work before?"

"There have been a few occasions over the years, usually only short trips. I don't often get the opportunity to spend time with friends while I'm here." He paused. "I'm glad I made an exception this time." The emphasis on his words left her in no doubt of his meaning. "I'm employed by an Australian owned multinational called Centian Corporation. Have you heard of them?"

She shook her head. "The name doesn't ring any bells. Do they have an office in Aurora Waters?"

"No. However the company does have a large pool of international resources. My main role is risk assessment and mitigation, but I'm really a glorified trouble shooter. Is that what you wanted to know?"

Nowhere near it. She was stumbling around in the dark. At least she had learned his employer's name. She could research the rest.

"It sounds like an important job. Do you have any meetings planned while you're here?"

"A few, but what about you? You haven't mentioned what you do for a living these days?"

"I have my own online business and I also help my mother with her party plan franchise. Plus, I do occasional contract work for a local company. Basically, I take work wherever I can find it."

"With all those commitments," his eyes widened with exaggerated admiration, "I'm not surprised you hesitated in joining me this evening. I'm flattered you took the time away from your busy schedule."

Just then, the waiter approached the table with their meals, distracting him before he had the opportunity to press any further about how she made a living.

Eli was a gifted athlete and popular personality at school, so it came as no surprise that he also proved to be an entertaining dinner companion. Amusing stories about eccentric teachers and badly behaved students had her in stitches, and by the time their coffees arrived, they were admiring the view and enjoying each other's company.

Having happily lost sight of why she had agreed to dinner in the first place, she made an abrupt return to reality when he tensed and shifted forward in his seat.

"I'm not sure what I anticipated when I extended the invitation to dinner, but I'm genuinely delighted with the way things have progressed. I don't want to spoil the evening, but there's something I need to confess."

"Confess?" Her growing confidence was shot to pieces by barbs of insecurity. So much for an evening of light-hearted reminiscences. His grim expression and rigid body language immediately reactivated her barriers.

"Let me know if I'm being tactless, but I can't help wondering how your health is these days. I heard the cancer returned after you finished high school."

That was a relief, she had imagined he intended to come clean about some sordid affair with Morgan Payne. She wasn't particularly comfortable talking about that part of her life, but he was probably only asking out of simple curiosity, or concern for her wellbeing. She couldn't fault him for that.

"I'm surprised you waited so long to ask. I don't like talking about it most of the time, but it's different with you. You were there at the beginning and you were always kind to me, unlike some people. I try to live a normal life and forget about it as much as possible." Not that her life was close to normal, but he wasn't to know that.

"You appear so healthy and well adjusted."

"I've been in remission this time for five years. Not that I'm counting." She stared out over the water, hoping he would take the hint.

"I'm happy things worked out for you. I can understand how you may dislike talking about it. After you were first diagnosed, I remember thinking how brave you were."

"I didn't have a lot of choice," she recalled. "I did what I needed to do to survive. That was all there was to it."

"Fighting for your life must have left you with some scars… not only physically… but psychologically.

Now she *did* feel uncomfortable. What was he getting at? "It hasn't been easy," she admitted, "but I try to take one day at a time. I think about it as little as possible, now you mention it."

The evening was deteriorating at a rapid pace, and after such a promising start, she felt a pang of disappointment.

"I'm sorry. I didn't mean to upset you. Tell me to go jump in the marina if you like."

His questions were leading somewhere, but she couldn't quite make the connection. Hoping that if she let her guard down, it might encourage him to do the same, she said, "I've been using bland clichés to describe my life for so long, it's almost second nature. I suppose it's because the more I talk about what happened, the more I think about it. It's easier to discuss it on a superficial level with most people."

"From an external perspective, no one would ever guess how much you've been through."

She acknowledged the compliment with an empty smile, resigned to the fact that no one except her psychologist was aware of the full extent of her inner demons.

"You're a beautiful woman Gemma. I hesitate to ask another potentially sensitive question, but how is it you're free to have dinner with me this evening?"

It was another abrupt change of topic. She wondered whether he was always like this, or if it was because he was eager to find out more about her life. She thought about Ryan and tried not to reveal how much the question had affected her.

"I'm not sure exactly what you're asking."

"I didn't mean to pry. My question was a clumsy way of discovering whether I have any competition. It's difficult to believe there's no one who would object to me sharing your company this evening."

"There *was* someone special. He moved to Melbourne for work, and we drifted apart." She would rather discuss her illness than her love life—or lack of it. "I date now and then, but I'm not seeing anyone at the moment."

Relieved when he changed the subject again, they reverted to the easy small talk of earlier in the evening. She was convinced he was hiding something, but she liked him anyway. He radiated the same warmth and charm that had attracted her in high school, and since he had matured, those qualities were even more magnetic than she recalled.

Dinner was over before she was ready. They were the last to leave and the waiter had been hinting for half an hour that it was time for them to move on. She hadn't learned anything about Eli and Morgan's connection, but it had been a fun evening, (aside from a slight detour down the memory lane of Hell Town), and she was glad she had accepted his invitation.

"Thank you so much for suggesting dinner. It's been really great to catch up."

"Does that mean you consider the evening to be over?"

"Does that mean you want it to continue somewhere else?"

"That was the plan. Unless you have more important things to do?"

"What did you have in mind?"

"It's a clear night, it would be a shame to waste all those romantic stars. Would you like to take a leisurely walk along the water's edge? I need more time to persuade you to see me again."

Why shouldn't she let him try to convince her? It didn't matter why Eli was back in town, or if he had seen Morgan. She didn't want the evening to end. "I guess it *would* be a waste. I'd like to spend a little more time staring at the stars with you."

At the waterfront a few minutes later, she noticed the stars weren't shining quite as brightly as before, like someone had turned down the lights with a dimmer switch. On hearing a familiar hum in the air, she clutched Eli's arm.

"Should I take that as a positive sign, or is something wrong?"

"I'm not feeling great." Her stomach felt queasy, so it wasn't a lie.

"That's a pity. I hope it wasn't the food. Do you want me to take you to the hospital?"

"No! No hospitals." A blur of movement in the shadows prompted her to tighten her grip on his arm.

"If a hospital is out of the question, wouldn't you prefer to go home to bed?"

"Not really. I don't want to be alone. Why don't we go to the Meridian? I can wait there for Bec to finish work. It's the perfect solution."

"If that's what you want, I'm happy to oblige."

•••

"Wow! They sure know how to treat their employees at that company of yours," she said, impressed by the extravagance of Eli's accommodation when they reached the Meridian. "This place looks bigger than my entire apartment."

"It's a corporate suite leased by Centian, usually reserved for members of the upper echelons. We mere mortals only get to use it if no one of importance needs it." He guided her to an impressive sofa. "Take a seat while I pour you a glass of water. Unless you'd prefer something a little sweeter… or stronger?"

"I'll stick to water. Thanks." Sinking into the sofa's billowy comfort, she ogled the luxurious surroundings while picturing her spoiled ragdoll shredding the plush padded arms and doing all sorts of unspeakable things to the custom-made shag pile rug. With so many scratch posts and snug spots to hide, Bones would be in feline heaven.

"Feeling better now?" he asked, as he handed her the water and took a seat next to her on the sofa.

"Much better, thank you. I was thinking about my cat. That's usually an encouraging sign."

Raising the glass to her lips, she watched helplessly as it slipped through her fingers and tumbled into Eli's lap.

Although her eyes tracked its descent in slow motion, she was powerless to stop it. Once the damage was done, her vision reverted to real time and she scrambled to retrieve the glass with one hand, while attempting to brush the spilled contents from his pants with the other.

With lightning reflexes and before she could do any more harm, he caught her wrists and pulled her hands from his lap. There was another second of stunned silence, then without saying a word, he righted the glass on the marble coffee table and left the room.

She was tempted to vanish into embarrassed oblivion while she had the chance but was more afraid of the unknown evil lurking in the streets than any awkwardness resulting from her clumsiness.

His pants were clearly expensive, and she was glad it had only been water in the glass. To make amends, she took a towel from the bathroom and mopped up the mess from the previously pristine sofa. The activity also allowed her to work off some nervous energy in the process.

Eli returned a few minutes later, wearing tight fitting jeans and a designer t-shirt. "Are you going to tell me what that was all about?"

"I'm sorry. I didn't do it on purpose. I must have been a little shaky… from before."

"If you don't want to explain what's going on, that's up to you. I'm not a fool. I can tell when someone is almost scared to death." He took her hand and traced his fingertips across her palm, generating a tingling sensation all the way up her arm.

"Someone attacked me in the street last Sunday," she blurted. "Then at the waterfront tonight, I got the feeling he was following us."

"Why didn't you tell me this earlier? A heads up at the time may have been useful. I get the impression you don't trust me Gemma."

"I'm sorry, I know I should have said something. I didn't want to spoil things." She buried her face in her hands.

"It's all right. No one can get to you here and you haven't spoiled anything. Have you contacted the police?"

"I went to the police station yesterday. A detective gave me his number and said to call him if the guy who attacked me ever showed up again. I'm not sure if a feeling counts, though."

"It may be important. You should call him anyway."

She wasn't sure if she was up to another conversation with Detective Vannen so soon, but she felt like she didn't have a choice.

He answered the call in his usual abrupt manner. "Yes, Ms. Glass. What now?"

"I think the creep who attacked me on Sunday was watching me tonight. I didn't actually see him, but after our last conversation, I thought I should let you know."

"When?"

"Twenty minutes ago. At Fairhaven Marina."

"Where are you now?"

"Uh… visiting a friend at the Meridian."

"Will you be returning to your apartment tonight?"

"If my friend doesn't mind, I'd feel better if I could sleep here tonight. Not that it's any of your business."

"In that case I won't offer a police vehicle to escort you home. I'll send a car to check out the marina. Thank you for your call, Ms. Glass. I'll be in contact if there's anything further to discuss."

She cringed at her stupidity. "That could have gone better," she said. "Do you mind that I invited myself to stay? I can sleep on the sofa."

"No need for that. You're welcome to sleep in the spare room. It sounds like you're not particularly fond of this Detective Vannen. Has he been giving you a hard time?"

"I suppose he's only doing his job, but he treats me as if *I'm* the one who's done something wrong."

"Have you?"

"What? No."

"Then you don't need to worry about him, do you?"

"I suppose not." It was comforting to finally have someone calm and rational on her side.

•••

A hoarse cry squeezed from her constricted throat as she bolted upright in the strange bed. Shivering with fear, every sense was on high alert, despite being alone in the darkness.

A lather of perspiration plastered her hair to her face and neck, and to alleviate the uncomfortable stickiness, she combed her fingers across her scalp. When long, damp tendrils came away in her hands, tangled like seaweed around her splayed fingers, she released one wretched sob into the suffocating darkness.

"Gemma! You're having a bad dream. Nothing can hurt you here." A soothing voice broke the threat of hysteria, and she woke to see Eli in the subdued glow of the bedside lamp.

A hesitant inspection of her hands revealed they were empty. Her eyes shifted to the bed, but there was only spotless white linen. Afraid of what she would find, she ran her fingers tentatively through her hair.

"Will you be all right? Do you need anything?"

"Another glass of water probably isn't a good idea," she said, trying to lighten the mood. "It was only a nightmare, but if you don't mind, I'll move to the sofa and watch television. I don't want to fall asleep again if I can help it." She didn't think she could take any more nightmares like that in one night.

"I'm happy to stay and keep you company. We can talk about whatever you like." He planted himself in the chair next to the bed and she couldn't help noticing his sexy sleep-tousled appearance.

"You don't have to do that. Honestly, I'll be OK."

"Do you remember that eccentric librarian who used to make us beg forgiveness of her books if we mistreated them?"

He seemed determined to distract her, and the question reminded her of a bizarre incident where she was ordered to drop to her knees in front of a science textbook. "Mrs. Emmanuel used to talk to her books more than her students," she recalled. "Poor thing. She definitely had issues."

In consideration of their shared past and Eli's generosity in allowing her to stay overnight, she felt she owed it to him to share more about the emotional impact of her cancer journey. "We all grew our hair long back then. I was convinced that I wouldn't lose it all, even though the doctor said I would."

"There's no need to explain. What you endured is enough to give anyone nightmares."

"I made it through chemo and radiation the first time with only a couple of minor long-term health complications. It was a rotten time for me, but it's easier to forget some things when you're young. When I relapsed, it was a different story. I'm still sensitive about my hair because it's a constant reminder of everything I went through."

Eli reached for her hand and it felt natural for him to hold it.

"I see a psychologist for PTSD. I thought I had it under control. But with everything that's been happening lately, I guess it's making a comeback."

"What else has happened?"

He had a habit of catching her off guard, and she withdrew her hand on the pretext of brushing hair from her face. She wanted to tell him everything, but the remnants of a nagging suspicion held her back.

"Some lunatic grabbing me and lurking in the bushes is bad enough—having to deal with Detective Vannen is almost as traumatic."

"Do you use flippancy as a deflection with everyone? Or is it only with me?"

"Most of the time it comes out before I can stop it. My therapist says it's a form of repression."

"You don't need to hide anything from me Gemma, I understand that you're different from most people."

She drew a startled breath, and he qualified the remark. "I meant I've never met anyone else quite like you. I thought it was a compliment. I didn't intend to offend."

An uncomfortable sensation made her lower her eyes. "I'm not offended, I just don't think I'm strong enough to cope with being different from everyone else. I hate the idea of standing out from the crowd. I wouldn't be surprised if that's the reason for the whole stalker thing."

He placed steady fingers beneath her chin and lifted her gaze to meet his. "Your strength and determination are what make you stand out, whether you admit it or not. How else would you have weathered the storm of everything that has happened to you? Stop being so hard on yourself. All you need is a little help to get you through this latest challenge. Will you do something for me?"

How could she refuse after everything he had done for her? "I guess I owe you," she said, wondering what she was getting herself into.

"Make an appointment with your therapist as soon as possible. You need to build your resilience in case of further incidents. I may not be around to help you the next time."

When she opened her eyes from a deep and thankfully dreamless sleep a few hours later, muted daylight leaked around the edges of densely woven curtains, providing just enough light to reveal that she was alone. By the time she made an appearance in the suite's living area,

Eli had already ordered a selection of food and beverage items from the room service menu; and although their conversation was stilted and slightly awkward after the previous night's disclosures, he insisted on seeing her home after breakfast.

On arrival at her apartment building, he accompanied her upstairs and continued to make small talk outside her door—clearly in no hurry to leave.

She wasn't in the mood for company and tried to hint as much, but he seemed determined to hang around. At first, she thought he was just being kind, but when a chilling thought struck her, she unlocked the door and raced inside.

Bones was at her feet before she had taken two steps into the narrow foyer, head butting her leg and mewling an extended protest to inform her that he was starving to death.

Eli followed her in, and while she tended to her ravenous ragdoll, he checked out her apartment.

"What made you drop everything and sprint through the door like that?"

"I got the idea you thought someone was inside."

"And that's what made you charge in with complete disregard for the consequences? Considering the events of last evening, don't you think that was a rather counterintuitive strategy?" There was an edge to his voice that she hadn't heard before.

"What about Bones?" She shrugged by way of explanation.

He shook his head. "What if the man who attacked you had been lying in wait with a weapon?"

"I didn't think of that. I had to make sure Bones was OK. Anyway, I have a sixth sense about that sort of thing. What if he *had* been inside with a weapon? What would you have done, hit him with your employee of the month plaque?"

The instant it came out of her mouth she regretted it. After everything he had done for her, it wasn't right to tease him about wanting to protect her.

"What indeed!" he replied.

Catching her wrists, he pinned them to her sides and propelled her back against the wall. It was an artful manipulation that required little effort on his part.

"As you can see, I have a few tricks up my sleeve."

Her physical reaction to his proximity surprised her. The warmth of his breath on her face and the weight of his body pressed against hers, was an intoxicating mix that she was powerless to resist. She made no effort to free herself from the close encounter, and when she didn't object, he lowered his mouth to the nape of her neck.

His sensuous lips nuzzled her responsive skin.

Having forgotten her arms were restrained until he released them, she draped them instinctively around his neck. After a few more delirious seconds where he explored the base of her throat with the tip of his tongue, his inquiring eyes met hers.

She encouraged him to continue what he had started with a flirtatious smile and he shifted his attention to her lips.

The pressure of his mouth on hers was firm and gentle, and the urgency of his kiss grew increasingly more demanding in keeping with her heightened response. In the heat of the moment, their lips parted… and an ultra-high-definition vision exploded inside her head.

Eli and Morgan were examining the interior of a unit at Palm Gardens. Morgan was unashamedly shooting lascivious glances in Eli's direction, but that wasn't the most disconcerting part. The unit was decorated in a distinctly masculine style, and there was a pack of playing cards and a small trophy lying in the middle of the dining table.

Snapping out of her daze, Gemma removed her arms from around Eli's neck and shoved her hands against his chest. The move didn't exert a great deal of force, but it did have the desired effect.

He promptly retreated. "I'm sorry, I shouldn't have done that. I know it was inexcusable, especially after everything you've been through. I promise I won't disturb you again. Take care of yourself Gemma." Turning his back on her, he walked out the door.

Stunned at the intensity of her reaction, (both to her vision and to Eli's sudden exit), she ran agitated fingers through her hair. Only moments earlier they had been entwined around his, and she regretted the impulsive reaction that had pushed him away.

He had been there for her when she needed him, and although she was angry, she wished she had given him the benefit of the doubt. There could be a genuine reason he wasn't able to tell her what he was doing with Morgan, she just couldn't imagine what it might be. She promised herself that if she ever saw him again, she would confront him about it.

Bones appeared the moment she was alone. "I can always rely on you, can't I Bobo?" she whispered, hoisting him into her arms and touching her cheek to his silky soft fur. His rapturous purrs were all the answer she needed.

CHAPTER NINE

After Eli's abrupt departure, Gemma was tempted to spend a few lazy hours stretched out on a towel at the beach. But considering her rent was due within the week, and her bank balance was currently insufficient to cover it, she fought the urge to de-stress and scanned her inbox for a straightforward location request.

A potential client wanted to know if *Gemini* could either locate a set of misplaced house keys or advise her on whether to go to the expense of having all her locks changed. It sounded easy enough, and this time she was ready when she skipped her usual transition and landed unceremoniously inside the family's trendy modern colonial.

During her astral tour of the rambling property, she found nothing that shed any light on the whereabouts of the keys, and she was almost ready to concede defeat when a curly haired munchkin skittered out of one of the bedrooms and vanished down the hall.

Chasing after the wobbly toddler, she arrived at the entrance to the kitchen just in time to see the little girl drop the keys into the rubbish bin. Then as if to highlight the cheekiness of her prank, the precocious child turned around and grinned straight at her.

Before Gemma could investigate the new development further, the sound of a familiar tune dragged her back to the cold reality of her apartment. She felt like the world was closing in on her and would have liked to create some emotional distance from it, but curiosity got the better of her, when she saw the caller ID on her ringing phone.

"How are you feeling this morning, Gemma?"

Detective Vannen called her Gemma—without prompting. He was being polite and asking after her wellbeing. She automatically assumed she was in trouble. "I'm fine Detective, what's wrong?"

"Why? Have you seen something?"

She thought about her vision of Eli and Morgan in Frank's room. "No. It was… you called me Gemma… and you're being friendly. It made me think there must be a problem."

"I'm sorry if using your given name caused you unnecessary concern. I was under the impression that was your preferred form of address."

"It was… I mean it is… forget I said anything. How can I help you Detective?" She gave up.

"The patrol discovered no one of interest at Fairhaven Marina last night."

"Oh, well thanks for checking it out. I'm not sure if that's good or bad. Is that all?"

"I have some other news. The information you provided enabled us to locate your grandmother's friend."

She closed her eyes in anticipation of what he was about to reveal. "Was I right? Was he dead?"

"You were correct in your assumption. Mr. Malloy is undeniably deceased."

The confirmation hit her hard, even though she had foreseen it. Her head grew fuzzy and flickered in and out a few times, and she was glad she was sitting down. "Wow. That was quick work. Can you tell me how he died?"

"I can't disclose specific details. The coroner hasn't completed her report as yet, and there are other issues that need to be resolved first. However, I can inform you that the probable cause of death was a heart attack, very likely initiated by trauma inflicted by one or more perpetrators."

"Oh my God! I can't believe this is happening." The memory of Frank's lifeless body resurfaced from the depths of her subconscious. "Was he at the house on Wattle Street?"

"Affirmative. Your description of the house led us to him. It's listed for rent and is currently unoccupied."

He had a way of stating the facts that made it sound like business as usual. Which she supposed it was—for him. Although her grandmother would be devastated, the outcome supported her decision to advise the police of her suspicions.

"There is *one* other thing," he continued. "I'll need to verify your whereabouts for last Sunday. The body was in the final stages of rigor mortis when it was recovered, and the coroner has estimated between late afternoon and mid evening on that particular day as the most likely window of death."

"You mean I'm a suspect?" The possibility had crossed her mind, but she hadn't seriously considered it.

"Given the early stage of our investigation, regrettably you are the main person of interest at this point."

Not only did she have a psychopath trying to kidnap her, now she was a suspect in a murder investigation.

"Do I need a lawyer?" She couldn't afford a lawyer, could she? She didn't even know how much they cost. She was certain Harvey would have one. He might help.

"It's doubtful whether you need to engage one at this stage. We already have your statement regarding your movements on the day in question. I'll let you know if we require any further information. If it turns out another formal interview is required, it may be in your best interest to retain legal representation at that point."

"Sounds fair. Hopefully it won't come to that."

"And Gemma…"

"What now?"

"Thank you for coming forward with the information. We may not have discovered Mr. Malloy's body for some time otherwise."

She wondered whether his thanks were supposed to be consolation for the fact that she had implicated herself in a police investigation.

"I'll be in touch." He hung up without waiting to hear her response. Not that she had one she was prepared to share with him.

Her first thought was that her parents would throw a fit if she didn't warn them. Taking a deep breath in expectation of the hysterics about to be unleashed, she rang her mother.

"Hello love. I was just about to call you."

It was that psychic gene again. Either that or mother's intuition.

"I have something to tell you."

"What is it? Have you seen Dr. Hudson? Do you have a temperature?"

"Nothing like that. Do you remember me telling you about Nan asking for my help to find her friend?"

"Yes, why? What happened?"

"Mr. Malloy is dead. Somebody killed him, and because I reported what I saw to the police, now I'm under suspicion." She waited for her mother's response under a cloud of dread.

"I knew something like this would happen."

She almost dropped her phone. "Why? How?"

"Nanna Glass told us everything. She thought something was wrong when she saw your reaction after you snapped out of your trance. Why didn't you tell us? We would have tried to help you."

She should have known her savvy grandmother wouldn't be so easily fooled. So much for not wanting to cause her additional grief. The urge to unload all her problems suddenly got the better of her. "Mum, there's something else I should tell you… but I'd better do it in person."

Both parents were waiting for her when she walked through their front door half an hour later.

"You'd better sit down and tell us everything from the beginning," her father ordered.

Like many of those employed in office-bound occupations, he had worked from home during the pandemic, and continued to do so for three out of the five days of his regular work schedule.

Deciding she had little choice, she came clean about almost everything that had happened since the lingerie party; only leaving out her ill-fated interlude with Eli and her suspicions about his connection to Palm Gardens. The last thing her parents needed to hear were the details of another potential relationship failure.

"Your mother will provide the particulars of everyone at her party, and they'll confirm that you were here for all those hours. I'm more concerned about some lunatic attacking you. It can't be connected to this Malloy's death, because it happened before you even knew about that. Why would anyone want to attack you, or be watching you at Fairhaven Marina?"

"I don't know. None of it makes any sense."

"It was lucky that Eli Nite was there. You couldn't ask for a better boyfriend than a football player at a time like this."

"Really Mum? Your aspiration for me is a football player? He's in town for work. It was a catch up—not a hook up. Were you listening at all?" Trust her mother to jump to conclusions.

"Didn't you work for Donovan Nite at one time Kris?"

"Back in the old days. Before Gemma came along."

She was surprised to hear that her mother had once worked for Eli's father, and made a mental note to ask her about it some time.

"What about that Ryan fellow you used to see? Have you heard from him lately?"

Her father never liked Ryan for some reason. Or was it only after he dumped her? She wasn't sure. "I haven't heard from Ryan in years. Besides, the creeper's voice was completely different."

"I wouldn't put anything past him. I never liked him at the time, and I don't like the idea of him now. If not him, who else could it be? It must have something to do with that website of yours. I knew it was a mistake doing that online psychic stuff. Who knows what sort of people you've been exposed to?"

He paused to take a breath and she jumped in before he went off on another rant. "Detective Vannen did suggest it could have something to do with my work. Sometimes people are disappointed when things don't work out the way they expect, but no one has ever made any threats. It's hard to believe anyone would actually hold a grudge."

"We'll have to leave that investigation up to the police to solve," her father conceded. "We should call your grandmother and find out what's happening there with the Malloy case. The police would have been to Palm Gardens by now. She probably knows more about what's going on than we do. Let me handle her."

He put Nan on speaker so everyone could listen in.

"I'm absolutely devastated Dougie. He was a dear man and such a splendid euchre partner. It won't be much fun around here without him. I knew young Gemma saw more than she let on, poor dear. I'm sorry sweetie, I had no idea Frank would turn up dead. I can't believe it."

"Don't worry Nan, you weren't to know. Sorry I fibbed to you. I didn't want to upset you unnecessarily. I hoped it was a mistake."

"Have the police been there?" her father asked.

"I thought I was in the middle of an episode of Sunset Homicide Squad. I haven't seen that much activity around here since silly Milly Henderson stripped off all her clothes and streaked around the dining room." Nan chuckled. "It took *ten* minutes for the staff to finally notice what she was up to, and another *five* to catch her."

"All right Mum—don't get side-tracked. Tell us what's happening." Patience had never been her father's strong suit. "What did they say happened to this Malloy?"

"They got us all together and made an announcement this morning. They said that Frank had passed away while visiting relatives. What a pile of crap."

Her father put his hand to his forehead as though trying to massage away an impending headache. "What else is going on?"

"There's police tape across the door to Frank's unit, and people in white jumpsuits have been coming and going all day. They carried away a lot of things from his room. Everyone knows something fishy is going on. We may be geriatrics, but we're not stupid."

Gemma could practically hear her brain ticking over.

"Then again, I suppose there *are* one or two who walk around with their wigs on backwards."

"Was there a tall detective with snowy hair?"

"As if anyone could miss him, sweetie. He and his partner were here for hours. He asked me about your visit. You know—when you went looking for Frank."

"What did you tell him?" She hoped it corresponded with the version she had given him.

"The truth. There was no reason to lie, was there?"

"Of course not, Mum." Her father leaned into the phone as if it would prompt Nan to get to the point. "What did you actually say?"

"That Gemma said she saw Frank… and that he wasn't up to much. I also told him that I knew she'd seen something dreadful. I could tell from her twitchy face. The detective is very tall, isn't he sweetie? There's been another cutie around here lately as well. He wears a suit and tie like the detective, only not so cheap. He's been talking to the residents and staff. I've seen him with Morgana le Fay a couple of times." A loud huff was clearly audible. "For a fancy pants like him to waste his time on trash like her, it must be something to do with work. Maybe she's finally going to get the boot."

Her mother and father were relieved that Nan was taking things in her stride and that the police had the investigation in hand. With those two worries out of the way, the next item on *their* agenda was to talk Gemma into moving back home until someone came up with a solution to her stalker dilemma.

As far as she was concerned, Nan had also confirmed her suspicions about Eli's visits to Palm Gardens. The jury was still out as to whether that was good or bad news.

CHAPTER TEN

Arriving early for her appointment at Clear Lakes Research Hospital, Gemma climbed the stairs of C Block to the second floor and hiked along the corridor to Suite 26.

A friendly face greeted her when she reached the front of the queue at reception. "How's it going Gemma?"

"Not bad Ben. How are you?"

"Excellent. Thanks for asking. Professor Eisen's running on time. You're next on her list."

"Good to know. I assumed I would have to wait awhile, considering it was a last-minute appointment." The quirky admin always went out of his way to be helpful when she needed an unscheduled session, and she rewarded his cheerful cooperation by enquiring about a topic she knew was close to his heart. "How's your garden Ben?"

"Outstanding. Thanks for asking. Did you know that every sunflower head is actually composed of hundreds of tiny flowers called florets?"

"Wow, is that right? You really know your flower stuff." Whenever he spouted the botanical Wikipedia at her, Gemma wasn't sure whether she was more fascinated by the content, or the quantity of precise detail that he remembered.

"There's a lot to know. I'm learning new facts all the time. Most people don't appreciate how complex flowers are, to say nothing of plant life in general."

"Are those some of yours?" She pointed to a vase of sunflowers at the end of the counter.

"How did you guess? Helianthus annuus, (or the common sunflower), is a member of the Asteraceae or Daisy plant family. Native to North America, they have a long history of cultivation dating back to

3000 BC. They were first introduced into Australia in the 1960s." Ben's round face beamed at her like one of his sunflowers.

"They're part of the Daisy family? What a coincidence."

"A coincidence? Sorry, I don't follow."

"I've been thinking about daisies a lot lately. Your sunflowers are some of the nicest I've seen. I should know, I buy a lot of them." It was hard not to be impressed by Ben's horticultural knowledge.

A rosy glow with the intensity of a sunset, seeped out from under the admin's white shirt collar. As it blasted up his neck to his cheeks, it accentuated his ruddy complexion, reminding Gemma of her late Great Aunt Iris and her crimson gerberas.

"Would you like to see my garden sometime? You'd like it," he said, peeping up at her like a puppy who thinks he's about to receive a treat.

It was her turn to be embarrassed. "Uh… that's very kind."

A woman waiting in line behind her, cleared her throat and saved her from planting herself in a romantic flower bed that she would need to dig herself out of. Shrugging her shoulders at Ben, she scampered out of the way and took a seat in the corner of the waiting room.

Not in the mood to make polite conversation with strangers, she made herself look busy by messaging Bec with an update of current events. Shortly afterwards, her phone rang.

"Hey Gem, your text sounded like you were on a bit of a downer. How would you like to hear me sing at the casino tonight? It might cheer you up."

"Finally, some good news. It couldn't have come at a better time."

"In the cocktail lounge around eight. Don't be late."

"I'll ask Deera and Lucky to tag along," she suggested. "I wish you would sing more often."

"Most of my usual gigs dried up thanks to that stupid virus. It's not easy jumping back on the treadmill once you fall off. Besides, hefty tips in the gaming room are easier to come by than what I'd make from slogging it out in the entertainment industry."

"With your talent, you should be touring the world."

"I get plenty of opportunity to show off my talent, don't you worry. Ask Connor about me singing in the shower. Besides, think about how much you'd miss me if I went back on the road."

"Hang on, as much as I'd love to hear about what you and Connor get up to in the shower, Harvey's trying to call me. I need to take it in case he has something for me. I'll see you tonight."

She crossed her fingers. "Hi Harvey. Do you have a job for me?"

"Something right up your alley G. Could be worth big bucks if things pan out."

"As long as it's not illegal or anything to do with missing persons, then I'm interested. I'm tied up for the next hour. Will you be free after that?"

"Not a problem. See you then."

Professor Jocelyn Eisen ushered her previous client through her door a few minutes later. After speaking briefly to Ben, she indicated with a cheery wave that she was ready for Gemma.

"Feel free to help yourself to a tea or coffee," she said, pointing to a refreshment table in the corner of her jumbled office. "There are some delicious choc-chip cookies today."

"I'm good thanks—big breakfast." Gemma claimed her usual comfy chair and the professor took a seat opposite her.

"How are you Gemma? You weren't due for your next appointment for another month."

"I've been better," she confessed. "I'm having nightmares again. A couple of things have happened lately that have got me pretty worried."

Her eyes wandered around the homely space and settled on a framed family portrait mounted on the wall behind the polished wooden desk. Her therapist's husband and two sons appeared to be clean-cut, outdoorsy types, whereas Jocelyn's homespun aesthetic was more suited to the kitchen than the bush. Gemma imagined them living in a rustic house, with two shaggy dogs and an untidy garden.

"Start by recounting the specific incidents of most concern."

With her attention refocused, Gemma described the attack and everything that followed, including her discovery of Frank's dead body.

While she spoke, she stopped herself from fidgeting by repeatedly twisting the rings she wore around her clammy fingers.

The professor allowed her to set her own pace, taking copious notes, and only responding once she finished speaking. "I see now why you requested an urgent appointment. It's understandable that the assault triggered acute psychological distress. Without a treatment plan, the effects could have proved disastrous in terms of your ongoing mental health issues. We'll return to that particular concern later. First, let's examine the other situation in more detail." Placing her pen and notebook in her lap, she fixed compassionate eyes on Gemma's face.

"The Frank Malloy situation you mean?"

"Your pursuit of a career as a psychic is understandably aligned with your desire to assert your independence from your family and the need for reassurance against further threat from your illness. It's normal to experience intense emotional and physical reactions following a traumatic event; they usually subside as part of the body's natural healing and recovery process. I have no doubt that you are an extremely sensitive person Gemma. However, I assumed that given time, you would rely less on this psychic persona. I believed it was a coping mechanism that would become less relevant as you resumed a healthier lifestyle. It's likely the attack has undermined many of your therapy gains."

Gemma was completely blindsided by the analysis, and in an effort to put both their minds at ease, she produced Detective Vannen's card.

"Please call this detective from Aurora Waters CIB. He'll confirm that I'm telling the truth. He didn't believe me at first either, but I'm sure he'll support my story now."

When the professor introduced herself to Alex and put the call on speaker, Gemma asked him to verify her involvement in the discovery of Frank Malloy's body.

"I'm sorry for doubting you Gemma," the professor said after speaking with him. "I associated your account of your vision with my preconceived ideas about your clinical history. I underestimated your uniqueness as a person. Please forgive me for not accepting the legitimacy of your enhanced extrasensory faculties earlier."

Gemma had never thought about her ability that way before. She wasn't a freak. She had "enhanced extrasensory faculties", like a very smart person, or someone with incredible reflexes.

"Recent developments are likely to have triggered the resurgence of your PTSD," the professor continued, "as a result, both past and present fears are manifesting in your dreams. Detective Vannen has a brusque communication style. Have your interactions with the police contributed to your anxiety?"

"Yes and no," she said, after giving the question due consideration. She explained that despite his intimidating personality, Alex had gone out of his way to be accommodating. He had answered all her calls, had never put her on hold or asked her to call him back, and had followed up promptly on every piece of information she had provided.

"I think I'm finally starting to get used to Detective Vannen," she said. "Thanks Professor, I can't believe how much better I feel. I'm so happy I came to see you."

"I'm glad the session has been of value Gemma. I hope you can forgive my initial reluctance to entertain the idea of a phenomenon which I admit is beyond the normal scope of my expertise. With all my years of study and clinical experience, I should have been more open minded with regard to the potential capacity of the human brain. Please feel free to call my direct line if you need to speak to me urgently. I can't pledge to be as accessible as Detective Vannen, however I assure you I will respond to your call as soon as possible."

On her way out, Gemma glanced at the reception desk and noticed Ben's eyes following her. Intent on sticking to her therapy plan, she considered making another appointment, but decided against it. If she was ever going to pay for her sessions without help from her parents, she didn't have time to listen to any more fun facts about flowers. She had work to do.

Lightning Bugg Investigation Agency occupied space in one of the oldest and ugliest high-rise structures in Aurora Waters. The hideous building's only redeeming features were that it was situated one block back from the esplanade, and she was eligible to use the employee parking in the basement.

The company name stood out in bold typeface on the agency door sign, while beneath it was a cartoon of a firefly squinting through a magnifying glass. It was a cute play on words—or so she thought until she met Harvey for the first time. After that it was just one more reason to spend as little time in his company as possible.

Harvey's bombshell office assistant acknowledged Gemma with her customary compilation of indecipherable words, followed by a tilt of her impeccable head towards the door to her employer's inner sanctum. That day, the gorgeous assistant's Cleopatra hairstyle was a flaming burgundy shade, and she wore fire engine red lipstick to match.

In contrast to what her name implied, Sunny projected an aloof and inscrutable personality that suggested she could care less about anything outside of her own reclusive world. Gemma wasn't even a blip on her radar from what she could tell, and she secretly questioned whether Sunny was a hologram, programmed to respond automatically to whoever came through the office door.

Uncomfortable turning her back on her, she wouldn't have been surprised if a viper's tongue had lashed out at her from behind as she slipped past her desk on the way to Harvey's door.

"What have you got for me?" she asked him by way of greeting after making it through his door unscathed. She was curious to discover what type of job had the potential to be so financially rewarding. If there was big money involved, she wanted to get started.

"Gemma, it's good to see you. Like I said on the phone, this one could pan out to be worth big bucks. Before we get to that, take a seat and make yourself comfortable."

Plonking her butt down on Harvey's dilapidated visitor's chair, she suppressed a smile. The firefly caricature depicted in the agency sign, stared back at her from the opposite side of his shoddy desk.

They say some people resemble their pets, or vice versa. Harvey Bugg resembled his name. He was short and thin, with a disproportionately large head, receding black hair and bulging eyes. If he had wings and an antenna sticking out of each temple he could easily have passed for the brother of the firefly in the cartoon. The comparison never failed to amuse her, but she had learned over the years not to underestimate him because of it.

"Sunny…," he called out in his squeaky insect voice, "bring Gemma a cup of tea."

"Uh, thanks for asking. A cup of tea would be great." Harvey could be annoying at times. She *did* like the tea though.

"I hear the cops have been putting you through the ringer."

"Where did you hear that?"

"I have my sources down at the station. Why didn't you call me after the slug tried to snatch you? I could have advised you on the best way to handle the legal ramifications."

Although the thought had crossed her mind at the time, she was reluctant to place too much faith in Harvey. But she couldn't tell *him* that.

Sunny arrived and set the tea down on the desk in front of her. Again, there was no eye contact or recognition of Gemma's presence, and she left as soundlessly as she entered. So much for the hologram theory. She was clearly an android.

"I didn't call you because I think I was still in denial. It took a while for it to sink in that it wasn't a mistake. Would you really have helped me out?" The tea was delicious. She kept meaning to ask what brand it was, but it always slipped her mind.

"Gemma, I'm offended." Harvey sometimes liked to pretend he had feelings. "What are friends for? Besides, you're an important asset. Course you can count on me if you need help. I'm always here for you—right?"

She was surprised to hear him acknowledge that she was an asset to his business. Even so, she was wary of becoming indebted. She thought of telling him about the shift in her abilities. "Before you tell me about the case, there's something else I need to discuss with you."

"Sure G, what's the problem?"

On second thought, she changed the subject instead. "Why did you give Lucas surveillance equipment? Has he been coming here? And if so, why?"

Harvey didn't even blink. "As I pointed out before, you're an important asset. Your brother made himself known to me. Said he was after part-time employment, so we negotiated a small job to ease him into things. He was keeping an eye on you for me. No harm in that, is there?"

She had always known there were other agency employees, but during the time she had been associated with Harvey, she had never met any of them except Sunny. Whenever she had asked him about it, he usually said something cryptic like, "They're all busy doing what they're paid to do. I wouldn't be in any hurry to meet any of them if I were you." After interacting with his rude office assistant, Gemma was inclined to follow his advice.

"Mum and dad would have a flat-out fit if they knew. I can't believe you got him to spy on his own family. That's a low move. No wonder Lucas is out of control. From now on, if you want me to keep working for you, leave my little brother out of the deal."

"Whatever you say, G."

He had agreed more readily than she had anticipated, which made her think he was up to something. If she hadn't been so desperate for the money, she would have told him where he could shove his agency. "What's going on with this case?" she asked.

"The client is Brandon Roth. His father passed a few weeks ago, leaving a multi-million-dollar estate. Brandon says his old man advised him shortly before his death that he had left the bulk of his estate to him. The old man's solicitor produced a will, but the girlfriend is named as the primary beneficiary."

"I'm guessing Brandon wants us to find the most recent will. What do you have for me?" Harvey would have sourced material likely to stimulate her sensitivity.

"There are a few options for you to try."

He extracted an envelope from his desk drawer, removed a stack of photographs from it and arranged some of them in front of her.

There was one of a distinguished man, (somewhere in his late seventies to early eighties), standing next to a curvy blonde who could easily pass for less than half his age. Harvey confirmed it was the dearly departed and his girlfriend. Another photo showed a forty-something version of the first man, who Harvey identified as Brandon. And lastly, there was a photo of an impressive mansion in one of Aurora Water's canal estates.

"Why wouldn't Mr. Roth's solicitor have a copy of the new will?"

"There are a few possibilities. Roth senior may have died before he got around to making the new will, or he made a new will and didn't get around to filing it with the solicitor…"

"Or the girlfriend and the solicitor are in it together," Gemma finished. "Then the new will is hidden somewhere, or it's been destroyed, or it may never have existed at all." Her dreams of easy money faded as quickly as the dollar signs in her eyes.

"Brandon intends to contest the will anyway, but he's sure his old man made a new one. He wants me to investigate the girlfriend and solicitor. If I uncover the missing will, he's prepared to pay me twenty grand on top of my other fees. Half of that is yours if you can locate it. Considering the estate runs into multi millions, it would be worth it to him."

Gemma understood her chances of finding the will were slim, but she couldn't resist the opportunity to make such a large amount of money in one hit. She collected the photos she thought would prove most useful, telling Harvey she would get back to him after she explored all the possibilities.

On the way out, she noticed a missed call from Detective Vannen. She was keen to get to work, and wasn't in the mood for further bad news, but couldn't bring herself to ignore him after his intervention with Professor Eisen.

"What now Detective? Are you going to arrest me?"

"Are you able to drop by the station this afternoon? Given my conversation with your therapist, I've decided it's time I shared some information with you about your case."

"I suppose so. Can't you tell me over the phone?"

"It's complicated. It would be easier to explain in person."

"All right. I'll be there soon." His reluctance to provide further details had made her curious, and she had forgotten to ask him *which* case.

CHAPTER ELEVEN

Leaving her car parked under Harvey's building, she set out to walk the two blocks to the police station via the esplanade. After her emotional rollercoaster morning, she hoped the cathartic mix of salt air and sunshine would help prepare her for another verbal onslaught by Detective Vannen. Making him wait a few more minutes would also be payback for how annoying he had been.

As she wandered along the esplanade, she watched the waves surge up the beach towards her. Bits of white lacy froth at the edges of the surf looked like millions of tiny eyeballs, staring at her as they tumbled over one another onto the sand. There was no mistaking the overwhelming sensation of spying eyes—all of them focused on her. Even the seagulls were fixated on her every move.

Determined to identify whoever was out to get her, she tuned in to the sights and sounds around her, hoping she would be enlightened by what Darshana had referred to as her inner spirit.

Traffic flow was sluggish, but there was nothing unusual about that. Cars often cruised the waterfront at ridiculously slow speeds in a bid to snag a parking spot.

The crowd of locals and holiday makers who packed the beach and alfresco dining areas appeared oblivious to everything around them. Nothing out of the ordinary in that either. No one seemed to be particularly interested in her as she raced along the busy pathway.

Except for one man. She had seen him at the hospital, and when she spotted him, he covered his face with a newspaper. Regretting the impulse that had brought her out into the open, she was ready to run into a shop or café to escape him if necessary.

But the closer she got to the station, the more the bad vibes fell away, and one last look over her shoulder as she darted into the building revealed her pursuer was nowhere in sight. She was certain she hadn't imagined him and assumed her proximity to the police station was responsible for his abrupt withdrawal.

Her previous face to face confrontation with Detective Vannen had been awkward, and she dreaded more unpleasant surprises. Unfortunately, one bad feeling was soon replaced by another.

"Thank you for coming in, Gemma. This is my associate, Detective Senior Constable Kelly."

The championship wrestling contender moonlighting as his partner, acknowledged Gemma with a curt nod as she took a seat opposite them in the interview room. Her eyes immediately descended on a bundle of paperwork in front of Alex. It was bulkier than she would have expected, and she was apprehensive about the type of information it contained.

"The purpose of this briefing is to bring you up to date with the progress of the two investigations in which you're currently involved. Before I begin, do you recall ever seeing this man before?" He removed a mugshot from a folder and slid it across the table in front of her.

"I think I would remember that face. Who is it?"

"There's a considerable amount of material to share," he said, stressing his next words, "please wait until I'm finished before asking questions."

"I can do that."

"By the time you attended the station to make your report, Detective Senior Constable Kelly and I were already in possession of dozens of photographs of your alleged assailant, taken while the attack was in progress."

"Wait—what?" the words exploded from her mouth before she could stop them, "How?"

"I explained you would have the opportunity to ask questions later."

She gawked at wrestler Kelly, only to be met by a blank wall. There was no help there, so she turned back to Alex. "You've been lying to me this whole time?"

"If you hear me out, the sequence of events will justify our reasons for withholding information from you."

"Go on." She doubted whether anything he could say would lessen her disgust.

"While the Japanese students were coming to your aid, some members of their group were taking photographs. After you left the scene, the teacher collected the evidence and reported the crime to police. We became involved when your assailant was identified as an alleged murderer who is currently on the run from police across two states."

He paused for a moment and Gemma took it as her queue to interrupt. "Who did he murder?" It was ridiculous to think she could sit there and not ask questions, especially with the type of information being thrown at her.

"I was getting to that. The suspect's name is Leon Ryder. It was his mugshot I asked you to identify. He absconded from Thornwood Prison in central New South Wales with another prisoner named Edward Bennett. They were on the run when Bennett was killed… allegedly by Ryder. Bennett's body washed up on the banks of the Mertree River a few weeks ago." He showed her another mugshot. "This is Bennett."

"Why would this Ryder kill him if they broke out of prison together?"

"We're not sure. After we identified Ryder in the photographs with you, we suspected you were connected in some way. It was plausible that you were either an accomplice in their escape from prison, or part of the reason Bennett was killed. When you failed to report the incident immediately, it only added weight to our suspicion."

"I guess I can see why you might think that. I was so scared about getting involved, I made things worse. Does all this mean I'm not under suspicion anymore?"

"After you identified yourself to us, we placed you under surveillance on the chance you would lead us to Ryder. When you called me about Frank Malloy, it complicated the case even further. Questions about whether you had anything to do with his demise—and whether he was associated with Ryder and Bennett—contributed to the puzzle."

"Why would I call you if I was involved? That doesn't make sense."

"I'm beginning to learn that nothing about you makes sense Ms. Glass."

"And are they connected?" She could hardly contain her curiosity.

"Frank Malloy had no criminal record, which on the surface precludes that assumption. We're continuing to dig into his background and the criminal histories of Ryder and Bennett. There is a lot of information to sift through."

As her brain worked to make sense of it all, she began to join the dots. "Were you having me followed the night I went to dinner with Eli?"

"In a way, yes. I instigated your meeting with Mr. Nite."

"Excuse me?" She felt like one of those clowns at the circus, with her mouth wide open and her head pivoting back and forth between the two detectives. Whatever happened to good cop—bad cop? She was urgently in need of a good cop. It was all too much.

"After you passed on the information about Frank Malloy, I spoke to the manager of Palm Gardens and she put me in touch with Mr. Nite."

Flurries of raging anger and burning embarrassment fought between each other to take control of her emotions. "I don't understand. Why would Eli have anything to do with Frank? He's someone I know from school."

"Eli Nite is the national security director for Centian Corporation, the company that owns Palm Gardens. He was investigating the whereabouts of Mr. Malloy on behalf of the corporation at the time and was aware you had been roaming around the village questioning staff about his disappearance. He was more than willing to keep an eye on you… and ultimately performed his role more thoroughly than I anticipated."

"Are you saying that Eli asked me out as a ploy to keep tabs on me?" She was still trying to make up her mind between embarrassment and anger.

"You would need to ask Mr. Nite whether he had any ulterior motives for agreeing to my plan. I can't speak for him. After I confirmed with him that Mr. Malloy was missing, I arranged a search of vacant houses meeting the criteria you outlined. As you know, we discovered his body shortly afterwards."

"You said I was no longer under suspicion. Why not?"

"After you identified yourself as the victim in an assault by Ryder, we conducted background checks on your family and known associates. Nothing led us to believe you were involved in either the manslaughter of Frank Malloy or the murder of Edward Bennett. Between Mr. Nite's report on your activities and our own observations, we have concluded that you are an unwitting victim of circumstances."

"It took you long enough." Her temper had reached boiling point.

"That is our initial conclusion. It's open to revision at any time. However, it is likely that your ability connects you to both cases. After further investigation, the association may become clearer."

"You mentioned Frank died of a heart attack because of trauma. I'm not sure if I really want to know more about how he died, but I won't be able to stop imagining possible scenarios until I find out exactly what happened."

"Is that the reason for the visit to your therapist?"

"Professor Eisen has been treating me for PTSD, among other things. You would know that anyway, after doing all those background checks on me. No wonder you answered my phone calls straight away. It all makes a lot more sense now. Here I was thinking you were so… efficient."

"I'm sorry about misleading you. I assure you it was necessary. As to Mr. Malloy, I'm not sure you would thank me for describing exactly what we found at the scene. He was secured to a chair in the vacant house in Wattle Street as you indicated. The coroner's report states that he died from a coronary spasm—a type of heart attack—in this case most likely due to the infliction of severe physical and possibly psychological torture."

Now she would have nightmares about her grandmother's friend being tortured.

"Your hands are shaking. Do you need a ride home?"

"I'm going to meet someone first. I assume you know I eat at Heavenly Spice a lot… since you've been officially stalking me. A friend of mine works there. Not that I'll be able to eat anything after hearing what happened to poor Frank. And before you say I told you so, I know I asked."

"There is one more thing before you go."

No… I can't deal with anything else. Don't tell me there's more. She stopped herself from shouting the words at him.

"I understand how stressful the last few days have been for you, however we'd like you to view photographs of the Malloy crime scene on the chance you can provide us with a lead in the investigation. There were no viable fingerprints at the scene and DNA results will take time. We don't have much else to go on at this stage."

How many times did she have to explain to these people that she didn't do that sort of thing? OK, she did it for her grandmother, but that was different. There was no telling what would happen. With the way her ability had changed recently, she didn't think it was the right time to try anything risky.

"I don't suppose either of you will get it, but I can't." Absentmindedly, she stared at a lock of her hair as she twisted it between her fingers. She already knew what Alex's reaction would be, and there was no way she wanted to see the look of disdain she assumed would be conspicuous on his offsider's face. "I'm sorry, I'd like to help."

"You're right. I don't *'get it'*, however I can't compel your cooperation." He closed the folder, linking his hands above it. "You've got my number. If you do come across any useful information, you know how to contact me. I'll see you out."

It was hard to believe that was all he had to say. She was of no further use, so she was being dismissed. He obviously couldn't care less about her safety or wellbeing.

Thinking about her safety reminded her of something. "There *is* one other thing I should mention before I go."

"Have you seen something relevant to the case?"

"There was someone following me today, but I don't think it was Leon Ryder."

Alex turned to his partner. "Rae, could you ask Constable Milne to join us please?"

Detective Kelly left the room and returned a few minutes later with the sneaky newspaper man from the esplanade. He was wearing a police uniform.

"I'm sorry if I scared you. I was supposed to keep an eye on you. I didn't think you would notice me in the middle of that crowd."

For someone who was supposed to keep an eye on her, he was having a lot of trouble looking her in the eye.

"Constable Milne followed you on my orders. We wanted to make sure you made it here safely."

She didn't know whether to be relieved or outraged. "And scaring me half to death is your way of protecting me?" she directed the question to Alex. She had to get out of there before she collapsed from emotional exhaustion.

Deciding to play it safe after her most recent fright, she caught a cab straight to the restaurant.

Deera was busy when she arrived, so she took a seat in their usual booth and called Bec. She needed to vent to someone. "Do you want to catch up for a late lunch? You can invite Deera personally to the casino tonight. I could do with some company right now."

"Are you OK Gem? You sound like you're on the verge."

"I'll be all right. I'll explain when you get here."

While she waited, she searched for information about Centian Corporation. She had been the subject of an investigation, now it was Eli's turn. If she ever saw him again, she wanted to know exactly who she was dealing with.

The information she found on his employer was basic, and Eli didn't have any easily accessible social media accounts. She hadn't discovered much in the way of useful information when Bec arrived. Deera finished with the lunch rush around the same time and they both took a seat in the booth.

"How are things going honey? Are you still under suspicion by the police?" Deera's voice was calm and soothing, but the frown lines above her eyes betrayed her concern.

"That's one thing I don't have to worry about anymore. Detective Vannen asked for my help to find Frank's murderer."

"I want to hear the juicy stuff," Bec said. "Don't keep us in suspense."

"The good news is that Professor Eisen acknowledged I'm not delusional… and the police don't think I killed Frank Malloy anymore."

"That's fantastic," Deera gushed.

"Now for the bad news. Detective Vannen knew who my attacker was the entire time he was interrogating me, Eli Nite works for the company that owns Palm Gardens, and I stayed in his suite at the Meridian the other night because the stalker came after me again."

"I can't believe you stayed overnight with Eli and didn't tell me," Bec said.

"I can't believe that's all you've got to say after everything I just told you." Gemma didn't know whether to be outraged or amused by Bec's total disregard for her mental anguish.

Deera screwed up her face like someone had spilled something disgusting on her best dress. "What a worm."

Gemma wasn't sure whether she meant Eli or Alex, but she was beyond caring. "Guess my luck with men is just running true to form. They either want to emotionally abuse me—or kill me."

Deera's hand jumped to her mouth. "It's all good," Gemma reassured her, "I was only joking. They were just doing their jobs. And even though Eli only asked me out because Detective Vannen suggested it, I'm glad he was around the other night. I don't know what would have happened if he hadn't been there."

"I'm sure you're right," Deera sighed. "You looked so amazing, it's a shame it was all wasted."

"Just because Eli was keeping tabs on me, doesn't mean he didn't enjoy having dinner with me." She wanted to believe it hadn't *all* been a charade.

"And he has a decadently luxurious suite at the Meridian… and you stayed the night in his suite. That's even more decadent." Bec was in fine form. Trust her to focus on a fictional sexual encounter.

"It was hardly romantic. I was scared half to death. It was the least he could do to let me stay, considering he was spying on me."

"Where did you sleep?" Now Bec had Deera hooked into her fantasy.

"There were two bedrooms. I slept in the one Eli *wasn't* sleeping in."

"Did Gemma tell you she had a crush on Eli at school, Deera?"

"*No…*" Deera dragged the word out until it echoed around the room, "she did not tell me anything of the sort. All she said was that he went to the same school as her. I should have guessed. I knew there was more to the story than she let on. That is *so* cute, I wish I had known when I was helping her get ready for the date. I would have taken much more care with her makeup and loaned her something sexier to wear."

"Don't you have to go back to work?" Gemma said, letting her friends know that she was over the conversation.

"I suppose I should take your order, otherwise I might get the sack." Her playful grin contradicted the idea that was ever likely to happen.

"Before you go, would you and Lucky like to escort lover-girl over there," Bec made a kiss face at Gemma, "to hear me sing at the casino tonight?"

"Please come with me Deera. I don't want to go alone," Gemma begged.

"Lucky will be working tonight, but I would adore it." Her musical laugh confirmed her enthusiasm for the arrangement before she zipped off to the kitchen with their orders.

•••

The Meridian cocktail lounge was already crowded when Gemma and Deera strolled through the doors from the sixth-floor foyer. They bought drinks at the bar, then with cocktails in hand, claimed two plush chairs on one side of a glass-topped table with their names on it.

Bec had reserved seats for them in front of the stage, where a middle-aged lounge singer was taking song requests at a baby grand. Two chairs opposite them remained vacant, and Gemma wondered if Bec had arranged for more of her friends to join them.

"You seem different tonight," Deera said. "I feel very dull compared to you. I didn't know it was possible for splits to go so high, or necklines so low."

Gemma glanced down at her black maxi. The boob tape was still keeping everything in place nicely. "You don't think it's too much, do you?" She had hoped a glamorous outfit would put her in a better frame of mind to enjoy the evening.

"It's good to see you dressed up for a change." Deera almost purred as she sipped her daiquiri. "Mmm, these cocktails are delicious."

"I'm only trying to live up to your standards."

"Thanks honey. I adore that pendant also. Is it new?"

"I've had it for ages." She stroked the tiny silver and gold charm that dangled from a fine chain around her neck. "I usually only wear it on special occasions, and there haven't been many of those lately."

"It's an unusual design." Deera inspected it more closely.

"It's a Roimata, the Maori word for teardrop. A friend of Mum's gave it to me when I relapsed. The blurb that came with it said it has something to do with healing and positive energy."

"It worked well for you the last time. With all this madness going on, let's hope it does its job again." She pointed to the stage. "The singer has finished, Bec must begin soon."

The piano man waited for the audience to show their appreciation before making an announcement. "Thank you friends, that's all from me for the time being. After a short break, the talented Ms. Rebecca Bowe will be joining us to perform for you. Please make sure to give her a warm welcome."

When the lights came up, Gemma scanned the crowd to see if she knew anyone, and her mood plummeted when she caught sight of a certain ex-classmate, perched on a stool at a high table near the bar. Morgan was at her voluptuous best, squeezed into a minuscule cocktail dress that left little to the imagination. She was alone, basking in the drooling attention of the men in her vicinity. Doubtless she had one of her many admirers in tow, and Gemma assumed he was at the bar, buying her the most expensive cocktail or bottle of champagne on the menu.

Was one night without drama too much to ask? She turned away, afraid the infuriating exhibitionist would spoil an otherwise pleasant evening.

"Isn't that woman over there the unpleasant one you used to go to school with? You know, the one who works at your grandmother's retirement village."

"Yes, unfortunately."

"The one you said has slept with every man on the coast. The one you call Morgasm behind her back." Deera made a sound low in her throat and Gemma couldn't be sure whether it signified delight or disapproval.

"That's her." She squirmed at her guileless friend's satisfaction at repeating everything she had ever blabbed about Morgan. "Act as if she's not there. That's what I'm doing." She pretended to inspect her fingernails.

"What is it with you two? Why do you hate each other so much?"

"I blame my parents. It's all their fault."

"Your parents?" If Deera's eyes had been bowling balls, they would have rolled right out of her head.

"I'm kidding. Although it did start with my parents in a way. They insisted I go to a different high school to all my friends. I was devastated. I thought spending the first year of high school without my closest friends would be the most disastrous thing that would ever happen to me. How wrong can you be?"

"That must have been very difficult for you."

"The new school wasn't as bad as I expected—it was the timing that sucked. First the separation from my friends, then I got sick. Facing two life-changing events at once wasn't easy. Add puberty to the mix and you've got a prescription for daily disaster."

"How awful." Deera's mercurial face grew more animated with each new detail.

"Then one day Morgan made a sarcastic comment about the scarf I wore to school after I lost my hair."

"What a nasty thing to do. I'm beginning to see what you don't like about that girl."

"Bec overheard what she said and took it on herself to get revenge. She swiped Morgan's school bag and coated the inside with dog poop. Naturally, Morgan went nuts and blamed me."

"Remind me never to get on Bec's bad side. And Morgan has held a grudge all these years over one poopy bag? That is ridiculous."

Gemma smiled. "No matter how much she scrubbed everything, she couldn't get the smell out of it. I'm talking gym uniform, lunch bag, books. She smelled like she had something stuck to the bottom of her shoe for weeks. After that I begged my mother to buy me a wig and Morgan hasn't stopped using it to insult me ever since. At the time it upset me. These days she's more annoying than anything."

"That's a long time to stay mad about such a little thing." Deera peeked in Morgan's direction.

"Don't look at her. She might see us. If she's got a half decent guy with her, she's likely to come over and try to rub my nose in it."

"It's too late. She has seen us, and she does have a fine-looking man with her." Deera sounded like a reporter for the local news.

Gemma wanted to check out Morgan's date, but refused to give her the satisfaction.

"They're coming over," Deera announced, "and he's not happy."

"If it isn't Aurora Waters' most renowned fashion icons." Morgan didn't try to hide her sarcastic tone. "Having a night out on the town ladies?"

Gemma wanted to ignore her, but she knew her childhood tormentor would continue to make snide remarks for as long as she held a captive audience. Frustrated, she raised her eyes to check out the latest victim of her debatable charms.

"Mor… Morgan. I see you brought a friend to hear Bec sing." She almost choked on the words, raising her glass to her lips to camouflage her reaction.

"You need to get your eyes checked, lovely. Surely you remember Eli Nite. Or has your memory deteriorated along with everything else?"

"It's a pleasure to see you again Gemma." After one probing look, he broke eye contact.

It took her a moment to recover her senses. "Deera," Gemma announced her friend's name a little too loudly, "I'm sure you remember me telling you about Morgan Payne. And this is Eli Nite. Eli was a few years ahead of us at Shellgarden High School."

"It's a pleasure to meet you Deera." Eli responded to her inquisitive gaze with a disarming smile.

"Nice to *finally* meet you too Eli," Deera replied, countering his smile with an enigmatic one of her own.

Morgan's shrewdness didn't run to subtlety, and she failed to catch Deera's veiled reference to Gemma and Eli's recent history.

"Now we've all been formally introduced, do you mind if we join your table? Eli and I popped out for a drink and who should we hear is performing tonight but our dear friend Bec. It's almost a school reunion, except for you Deera. Anyway, I'm sure it will still be lots of fun."

"Of course, you're welcome to join us. Have a seat," Deera answered on their behalf.

Dumbfounded, Gemma watched Eli and Morgan settle into the chairs opposite them. The lights and background music faded almost simultaneously, the spotlight came up, and the piano man returned to his place at the baby grand.

He leaned into the microphone. "Please put your hands together for Ms. Rebecca Bowe."

At the sound of her name, Bec floated onto the stage. Her platinum blonde hair was curled to frame her elfin face, and she wore a sequined amethyst evening gown that perfectly matched the shade of her bellflower eyes. Her appearance prompted a spontaneous burst of applause, and even before the first breathy notes left her mouth, the audience was spellbound.

Despite the dim lighting and repeated attempts to block out the couple on the opposite side of the table, Gemma wasn't able to enjoy Bec's performance. Her eyes had a mind of their own, wandering in their direction without her consent. Morgan made the most of the opportunity to flaunt her relationship with Eli, and even from the other side of the table, it was evident her hand was strategically positioned on his leg.

Gemma wondered why he would indulge in such blatant flirtation in front of her. Was it revenge for pushing him away? Or was this the *real* Eli Nite she was finally seeing?

Distracted by Morgan's dirty tricks, she was missing the one positive experience she had hoped would save her week from turning into a complete disaster. To prevent an overreaction that she knew she would regret later, she chose to escape the situation before she made a fool of herself. Deera and Bec would be disappointed, but they would understand after she explained.

Before leaving the table, she whispered an excuse in Deera's ear. Self-conscious about her emotional state, she counted on the low light in the lounge to mask her distress. Thoughts of Morgan and Eli's intimacy had provoked the threat of tears, and to avoid inquisitive eyes in the glaring lights of the foyer, she hurried into the lift with her head down.

The unpleasant scene had distorted her perception, closing her off from what was happening around her, and once removed from it, her head cleared. When the lift door opened in the basement, she was engulfed by an overpowering sense of vulnerability. The impending doom that had haunted her for days had returned, erupting from the depths of her subconscious to invade every prickling cell of her body.

CHAPTER TWELVE

Her restricted view of the crypt-like garage revealed nothing to imply she was in any imminent danger. There were no signs of her skulking stalker, and the thought of returning to the cocktail lounge was more daunting than the latent malice she sensed. Choosing what she hoped was the lesser of two evils, she ran for her car as fast as her perilously high heels would allow.

When she reached it she was shaking, and she fumbled the key into the lock, cursing her lack of central locking.

"Don't move." A scruffy beard couldn't disguise Leon Ryder's mugshot face as he emerged from behind a concrete pillar and pointed a gun at her. He ripped her phone and keys from her hands and tossed them away. Then edging behind her, he rammed the muzzle of a gun into the small of her back.

"What do you want?" She shot a pleading look at one of the security cameras.

"Shut up. Make another sound and I'll kill you." He pointed at a dusty blue sedan. "You and me are going for a little ride in the country. Hurry up or you'll cop a whack in the face."

Despite his threats to hit her, she obeyed as slowly as a procession of painful jabs in her spine would allow, praying that someone would see what was happening before she disappeared off the face of the earth forever. She was convinced that her friends, (or even Eli), would come to her rescue if she could delay long enough, but within seconds the car was already speeding off with her locked away inside, out of sight of curious eyes.

Ryder raced for the exit around the winding turns of the garage, and with every muscle tensed, she was repeatedly slammed against the hard interior of the compact compartment. When they reached the street, the car found its level, and it was only then that she remembered what she'd heard about an emergency lid release. There was supposed to be a lever somewhere.

By the time she found it—it was too late. He stopped the car, leaving the engine running while he stomped around to the rear end. "I'm going to tie you up, so you don't get any ideas."

"You don't need to do that. I won't try anything." From the little she could see, it appeared as though he had pulled off a side street into an alley.

"After last time, I'm not about to take any chances. Follow instructions and you might save yourself a few bruises." He secured her wrists and ankles with cable ties and gagged her with a greasy rag. "If I hear a sound out of you in here, I'll pull over and shoot you, no questions asked. Do you understand?"

There was a cruel twist to his mouth that warned her to take him seriously. She nodded, and his screwy smile was the last thing she saw before he slammed the lid down on top of her again.

For a few frenzied minutes she tried to loosen the ties, thrashing around like a dolphin tangled in a shark net inside the confined space. They wouldn't budge, so she conserved her energy. With her hands and feet out of action, she wasn't prepared to risk a bullet to the head for a minimal chance at escape from a moving vehicle.

The car climbed steadily for what felt like eons after leaving the stop-start of the city behind, and the next time it came to a standstill, he killed the engine. Judging by the slope of their ascent and the amount of time that had passed, she guessed they were somewhere in the Aurora Waters hinterland.

Her ears strained to hear something that would suggest what was about to happen, and when the lock clicked open, she imagined his rough hands tightening around her throat. She choked back a scream. Her eyes had already adjusted to the gloom, and there was no mistaking the outline of the figure standing over her. Behind him, slivers of yellow light leaked through the ramshackle walls of a dilapidated farm building, and she wondered if someone was waiting for them inside.

He removed her gag and cut the tie around her ankles with a knife. The impulse to run intermittently flickered in her scrambled brain, but she overruled it. Her muscles were rigid with cramp and tension. He had already killed someone, and she didn't want to be the next notch on his belt.

She recoiled as he gripped her arm and stuck the point of the gun into her spine. "You don't have to do that. I swear I won't run."

"If you scream, no one will hear you. You'll only piss me off. If you try to run, you'll be dead before you reach the road. I guarantee it." A snickering snort spewed from his throat and nose, as if he enjoyed the thought of shooting her.

It turned out running wasn't a viable option anyway. She had to force her puppet limbs to work in unison as she stumbled into the old shed. High heels didn't lend themselves to efficient movement at the best of times, let alone on uneven ground with cramped legs. Until she devised a plan of escape with at least a slight chance of success, she hoped it was in her best interests to follow instructions. For the time being she would settle for having his hands off her and the weapon away from her body.

An oil lantern perched on a wooden table emerged as the light source inside the shed, and aside from a few other pieces of mismatched furniture and some rusted farm machinery, the interior was mostly empty.

Sliding the gun into his belt alongside the knife, he picked up more ties from the table and secured her arms and legs to one of the spindly chairs.

While he worked, she studied his bristly face, and what she saw discouraged her from attempting to make friendly conversation. He didn't look like the chatty type. She wanted to demand he let her go, but she was at his mercy and didn't dare provoke a response she wasn't prepared to handle.

"Right," he unnerved her with a gap-toothed grin, "now I know you're not going anywhere, we can get down to work."

"What sort of work?"

"I want you to find something for me, *Gemini.*" He hissed the name at her like a childish taunt.

"My name's not Gemini. And I don't know how you think I can find anything for you when I'm tied to a chair."

"Shut up until I tell you to talk." He shoved a battered snapshot under her nose. "Here's the double-crossing weasel who stole my money. Take a gander at his ugly dial and tell me where to find it."

She had seen Edward Bennett's face during Detective Vannen's briefing. He had two distinctive tattoos: one under his left eye that looked like an ancient tribal marking, and another of a knife along his jawline below his right ear. The inky accessories were almost as intimidating as his aggressive expression, and they would give her something specific to focus on.

"You want me to find the location of some money stolen by this man?"

"It's not just *some* money, it's *my* money. He owed it to me. So, make it quick or you'll regret it."

The way Ryder's eyes glittered in the lamplight reminded her of a rabid animal preparing to pounce. She was wary of inflaming his anger any more than necessary. "Can you please untie my hands? It works better that way."

He thought about it before replying, looking her up and down with a condescending sneer. "Don't do something stupid and make me hurt you. There are other ways I can kill you that wouldn't be as quick or as painless as a bullet." He released her hands, leaving her ankles tied to the chair.

Rather than think about the multitude of ways he could kill her, she focused on the photograph.

Bennett's face disappeared the moment she closed her eyes, reminiscent of her attempt to locate Frank. When she opened them again, she was surrounded by dense bushland. The vegetation and terrain were comparable to state forests she'd trudged through on bushwalking trips with her family as a child. There were several within a few hours' drive of Aurora Waters, but there were no visible signs or landmarks to indicate which one she had projected into. Above the soaring canopy, all she saw were sparse patches of blue.

The sensation of someone breathing down her neck was more pronounced than she had expected, and it was difficult to concentrate knowing she was under intense scrutiny. It wasn't likely Ryder would hurt her while she was doing what he asked, but she didn't rate her chances of surviving his temper for long if she failed to find something quickly. Even then, her fate was questionable.

As her eyes skimmed the ground between the trees, a fuzzy patch of dirt and leaves immediately grabbed her attention, standing out from the rest of the leaf litter because of the shimmering haze that surrounded it. On closer inspection, she discovered the outline of a strange hybrid animal carved into the mottled bark of a giant gum behind it. The freaky depiction fused the head of a bird with the tail of a fish—one of the less appealing creature concoctions she had ever seen.

Centaurs definitely had a lot more going for them in terms of sex appeal.

Another fragment of haze suspended above the ground at eye level, directed her to a different carving of a circle with an arrow through the middle. The presence of the two symbols hinted that she was on the right track but told her little else of value. They could be signs pointing the way to the loot, or indications that some odd ritual had been performed in the area, or stupid figments of her imagination that had no relevant meaning whatsoever. Whatever they were, they were useless to her without additional context.

If the hunt for the money turned out to be some type of lateral thinking puzzle or IQ test, she was screwed. Solving riddles and cryptic crosswords had never been her strong suit.

With the discovery of the carvings, the hostile aura around her grew more intimidating. At first she was convinced it originated with Ryder, because no one in the psychic realm had ever reacted to her presence before, but then she remembered that the toddler with the keys had looked right at her.

While she racked her brain over the meaning of the second carving, an unearthly fog oozed out from between the trees. Faced by a choice between vaporous atmosphere and a tangible gun, she stood her ground, gambling that the fate waiting for her at Ryder's hands would be far worse than anything a creepy cloud of mist could do.

Before she could reconsider the decision, glacial tendrils swirled around her astral body, freezing her in place. Literally petrified, she only avoided becoming a life-sized ice sculpture thanks to a hot zone in the middle of her chest that prevented the cold from rising any further.

It gradually dawned on her that the shield of warmth around her heart radiated from the spot where the Roimata rested against the skin of her corporeal form.

Once she was trapped, a familiar face emerged from the fog. The cadaverous features scared her so badly, her mind exploded in a piercing telepathic scream. The phantom replied with his own spine-chilling screech, and the more she screamed the angrier he became, responding with one shriek of rage after another.

Bennett's ghost was guarding his treasure from the grave, and the ghoulish reaction was only the beginning of a transformation that became more insane by the second.

With the strain of each tormented howl, the bulging purple veins in the apparition's neck erupted in a mass of tar-like sludge. As the oozing mess spread down over his shoulders and up his neck to cover his entire head, his nose expanded until it protruded from his face like a beak, and his thick black hair disintegrated, replaced by speckled feathers that sprouted from his skull and upper body.

The process was gross to watch, and the whole time Gemma was transfixed by the obscene mutation, the creature was fixated on her as if it wanted to peck her eyes out.

While Bennett's top half turned into the head of a bird, exactly what was happening to the rest of his body was hard to tell. She was grateful the fog shrouded his nether regions—that was *one* refit she wasn't keen to watch. The bizarre anatomical renovation of the upper level suggested that the rest of his body had changed into the bottom half of the hybrid animal.

But the metamorphosis didn't stop there.

As the creature's beak continued to expand, simultaneously growing increasingly rounder, the plumage and lower body parts dissolved into the fog. The figure of the bird-fish gradually completed its transformation by devolving into the shape of the circle symbol—minus the arrow.

With the threat extinct, Gemma congratulated herself for facing down the evil entity. Although she couldn't have broken free anyway, she was proud of the way she had handled the situation. What were a few screams between mortal enemies? If only she could work out how to thaw out, she could resume the search for the hidden money.

Thinking about the cash was a mistake. The circle started to spin the moment the thought crossed her mind, whirling faster and more furiously with every rotation. The speed and ferocity of the previously benign orifice escalated to form a mini tornado, with a raging ice storm lashing out at her from its core. The stabbing pain was excruciating, and the more she struggled against it, the deeper it pulled her into the churning chaos of the vortex closing in around her.

The moment she closed her mind to the hammering darkness, her consciousness returned to the derelict building, and the arrows of ice that had afflicted her astral body were revealed as the point of Ryder's gun. The pressure of the cold metal against her skin dragged her out of her trance as he repeatedly jabbed it into the flesh of her arms.

She had gone from one nightmare to another, and she wasn't sure which was scarier.

"Shut up you stupid bitch. You better have something to tell me because I've had about enough of you."

"I found the place." She said it without thinking, so he would stop hurting her.

He calmed down immediately. Still waving the gun, he took a step back, a smug smile chasing away his anger. "Well? Hurry up and tell me. Where is it?"

She was in shock, and her next words brought immediate consequences. "I don't know exactly. I think it's buried in a state forest somewhere."

Before she had time to rethink her reply, his hand launched at her head. His open-handed slap connected with her face, sending her flying sideways, and with her ankles tied to the chair she had no way of controlling the momentum of the fall. She landed with a sickening thud, smashing her head against hard packed earth.

•••

Eli watched Deera squirm. In between countless checks of her phone, her anxious eyes darted around the room. Gemma had been gone too long, and she wasn't the only one concerned. He had the feeling be should have been more diligent about curbing Morgan's rash conduct in public.

Following multiple encores, Bec took her final bow and approached their table. "Where's Gemma? I saw her leave. It's not like her to walk out during one of my performances. Did she say where she was going?" The question was aimed at Deera.

"To the restroom. If only I had gone with her. I went to look for her, but she's not there. She's not answering my messages. Would someone please come with me to check her car?"

"Don't waste your time. She's just throwing one of her sulky turns. You know how she is." Morgan attempted to draw the group's attention back to herself, as she was prone to do.

Bec was having none of it. "What are you doing here Morgan? Shouldn't you be busy working a street corner somewhere?"

"Eli and I were looking for entertainment. It's a pity we haven't been able to find any. You remember Eli, don't you?"

Bec turned audacious eyes his way and hurled her next pointed question at him. "Gemma said you were back. Where is she?"

CHAPTER THIRTEEN

She saw herself sprawled in a tangled mess on the dirt floor. If there had been breath in her astral body, she would have held it as Ryder checked her pulse and removed the ties that still bound her ankles to the legs of the chair.

He laid her out flat on her back and retied her hands and feet. When she was secure, he spread a map on the table and flicked an occasional glance at her unconscious figure as he studied it.

While her fate rested in the hands of the monster below, she floated in an atmospheric bubble above the daunting spectacle, only the second time she had ever astral projected while unconscious.

The day of her stem cell transplant, Ryan had promised to visit her in the hospital. Instead, he called to tell her that he had been offered a job in Melbourne requiring his immediate relocation.

Shortly after receiving the news, her frail body was overcome by a fit of shakes, her vision blurred, and the hospital room and everyone in it faded away to nothing.

The blare of alarms and emphatic voices lured her back from the brink of nothingness.

Reflecting on the scene below, it was almost impossible to believe that it was her body the medical team were trying to revive. The gaunt, bald creature, surrounded by a profusion of plastic tubes and blinking lights, looked more like a refugee from Area 51 than a critically ill human being on the verge of death.

All that connected her to the chaotic scene playing out beneath her was one tenuous thread of life. She felt no sense of loss or urgency, just detached curiosity.

"Why so sad, kiddo?" The voice invading her thoughts sounded like her grandfather.

"Pop, is that you?"

"Who else would it be? Father Christmas? Ho-ho-ho."

She suspected her mind was playing tricks on her, but it sounded like one of her grandfather's jokes. "What's happening Pop?"

"That's what I'm trying to find out. Do you intend to explain or not?"

As she chatted with the voice in her head, she kept an eye on the commotion around her hospital bed. "I think I'm dreaming. I had a stem cell transplant, and for a while everything seemed to be working the way the doctors said it would. Then next thing I knew, I was freezing to death. I went unconscious… and now here I am."

"Hmm. You've had a rough time, you poor kid."

"My life is over. Not that I care anymore." She was ready to give up.

"That's enough of that kind of talk." Pop had never been one to put up with defeatist language. "What happened to upset you like this? Why would you give up now when you've come so far? The Gem I know is a fighter—not a quitter."

"Didn't you see what happened?"

"I have eight grandchildren. I can't keep an eye on *all* of you all the time. You've kept me busy enough lately as it is."

The idea that he had been watching over her all this time, was almost as spooky as having just joined him. Or had he joined her? She wasn't sure.

"There's nothing much to tell. I guess I went into shock or something."

It felt strange talking to a disembodied voice. Like using her phone on speaker, only without the phone. The sound seemed to be coming from everywhere and nowhere all at once.

"And… what brought this crisis about? Why the tears?"

"My boyfriend is moving to Melbourne. I know I'm never going to see him again. Without him, I have nothing else to live for." A thought struck her. "Am I already dead? Is that why you're here?"

Pop chuckled. "You're a rare gem, as indestructible as your namesake. When has anyone ever been able to get you to do something you didn't want to do? You're the most bull-headed of all my grandchildren. You remind me of me."

While she drifted aimlessly above the drama, her mother stood rigidly at the back of the hospital room, teary eyes fixed on the emergency unfolding in front of her. She looked half out of her mind with fear, and Gemma wished she could console her.

"It would be beaut if you decided to join us. Ida would love to see you again. She never stops talking about you. You have such a big heart Gem… you were always very special to her."

"Is Aunt Ida with you?"

She pictured her grandfather and great aunt, sitting at an ornate gold table surrounded by a froth of fluffy white clouds. Aunt Ida added six teaspoons of sugar to ambrosial tea, while Pop read the heavenly news, stuffed himself with angel's food cake, and pretended not to notice.

The sound of gentle laughter interrupted her fanciful view of Heaven, as if he could tell what she was thinking.

"Yes, Ida is here, and she's still fanatical about gerberas and cats. There are certain things about a soul that never change. Our most precious memories are always with us. All my old army mates are here too. They'll appreciate having you around. It's a pity your mother and father will miss you so badly… and Lucas will get into plenty of trouble without you to keep an eye on him. But if you've really had enough, then I won't try to talk you out of it."

The idea of leaving behind the pain of her illness and the heartache of losing Ryan was tempting, but it would also mean she would never be able to speak to her mother and father again. They had promised to buy her a kitten, and her mother needed her help with Lucas. What if the stem cell transplant worked? There were so many possibilities she wanted to explore, even without the love of her life.

"You're not ready to let go yet Gem, but don't worry, I'll be here to welcome you when you are." Pop had read her mind again. "I want you to take care of your grandmother for me, and there's someone else who will need your help in the future. You're going through a rough patch right now, but you'll get through it. One day you'll learn just how special you are, and when you do, nothing will be able to stop you. Keep following the sun my little sunflower. And whenever it's not shining... I'll be there."

She felt the flutter of a gentle kiss on her forehead, and he was gone.

Thinking back on it, she couldn't believe how close she had come to giving up. The doctor said it had been touch-and-go, and even years later her mother couldn't bear to talk about it. She had convinced herself that the surreal episode had been a dream. Now she wasn't so sure. It appeared to be happening again, only her grandfather wasn't there to reassure her.

Seeing her vulnerable body lying exposed to the vile temper of Leon Ryder was all the incentive she needed to find a way out of the mess she was in. Desperate to avoid the situation while searching for a means of escape, she imagined what it would be like to roam wherever on earth she wanted. Anything would be better than observing her current predicament.

Blocking out the confronting sight below, she pictured herself carried along through tranquil skies on a ripple of starlight.

The transition was effortless. In a blink she was free of the old shed, with a bird's eye view of its battered tin roof.

Far above the clustered lights of the coast, the stars glowed brighter, sparkling with the intensity of tiny jewels. Their sheer multitude overwhelmed her, like she was drifting in a cosmic ocean, with a spectacular star scape above and night lit scenery below. In the distance she picked out the lights of the city and followed the iridescent cobweb trails as they branched out from its heart.

It was comforting to know she wasn't far from home. All she had to do was find a way to get her body back there in one piece.

Being so far above the ground was a different proposition to hovering over a hospital bed. She would have preferred to experiment more with her newfound ability before trying something drastic, but the fate waiting for her at Ryder's hands was a lot scarier than hanging around in the stratosphere. She had to take the chance that it wasn't all a dream and find a way to identify the location of the property where she was being held.

Reading the local street signs was her first idea, but she rejected it. Since she had first driven Pop's zippy Hyundai, she had steered the wrong way down more one-way streets than she was ever likely to admit, even with the benefit of satellite navigation. Considering her poor sense of direction, the use of landmarks of any kind would have to be a last resort.

A rustic farmhouse nestled on the side of the next hill looked like a far better proposition, and following the same process as before, she pictured herself inside it.

When nothing happened, she concentrated on the sky above the house instead. But that didn't work either.

Assuming there was a trick to astral travel in her current condition that was eluding her, she wished she had done some research after her first experience. A copy of Astral Travel for Dummies would have come in very handy at that point.

There was clearly someone living at the property. Lambent light spilled through two lower floor windows, gently illuminating the surrounding countryside. She wondered which room was occupied so late at night, and the instant her focus shifted to the source of the light—she was there.

Inside the farmhouse's roomy kitchen, an incandescent globe wrapped in a stained-glass shade, dangled above the heads of an elderly couple sharing a late-night snack.

The woman shivered and rubbed her hands up and down her arms. "Reg, did you feel that?"

"What are you talking about Flo? You must be imagining things. I didn't feel anything."

Flo blinked, then peered around the room with screwed up eyes. "I dunno, I thought I felt something. It doesn't matter. I'm tired. It's been a long day. We need to go to bed, or we won't want to get up in the morning."

Not relishing the idea of being left alone in the dark, Gemma scoured the kitchen for anything that would provide a clue to the location of the old farm building. Resting on top of an age-worn sideboard, she discovered a postmarked envelope with an address on it.

•••

"The suspect's name is Leon Ryder. We were able to identify him, and the registration number of his stolen car, from security footage. There have been no sightings since we issued the bulletin, so we assume he's hiding out with her. They could be anywhere within a two-hour radius by now."

No one had so much as blinked when Gemma had dropped in on Alex and the others in a meeting room at the Meridian. It had taken a while to find them, and if that was their only progress, she was in trouble.

"What possible motive could this Ryder have?" Eli asked.

"One theory is that it has something to do with what she does for a living."

"As if anyone in their right mind would believe all that psychic rubbish," Morgan chimed in. "Maybe someone finally took her seriously. That's what she gets for being a fake."

There was no change in Eli's expression after Morgan's disclosure concerning her occupation, and Gemma wondered whether he already knew.

"That's a laugh coming from you," Bec snarled. "I hear you're operating with a few parts that aren't exactly one hundred percent Australian made and owned these days."

Alex interrupted before the squabble could escalate. "Whatever his motivation, Ryder is a dangerous fugitive. If anyone here knows anything they think might help, now is the time to mention it. He's currently the main suspect in a murder investigation."

Deera sucked in a breath and Bec threw an arm around her. "Hold it together Deera. She's survived worse than this."

Gemma wanted her to be right, but Bec didn't fool her, she was as worried as everyone else.

Everyone except Morgan that was. "I don't know what you're so upset about, she's obviously doing it for attention. That's why she started all that psychic rot, she loves playing the damsel in distress… has done since high school. If it's not cancer—it's being kidnapped."

"If you don't shut your troll mouth, I'm going to punch you in your pointy little nose until it's bigger than it was before you had it trimmed." Bec spat the words in Morgan's face and Gemma had no doubt she would do it.

"She's just jealous because Eli and me are together." Morgan took a step backwards before making one last vicious suggestion. "She probably set the whole thing up herself."

That was all the incentive Bec needed, and she lunged at Morgan with closed fists.

Alex grabbed her arms before she managed to land a blow.

"Don't be ridiculous," Eli fumed. "From now on, don't say another word unless Detective Vannen asks you a question."

Gemma would have laughed aloud if she could have.

"Why am I being ridiculous? What about *us?*"

"There is no *us*. There never has been and there never will be. You are an employee of Centian Corporation, and someone I used to go to school with—end of story. Do you understand?"

Morgan opened her mouth as if to say something, then snapped it shut again. Her eyes flashed fire before her lashes swooped down to cover them, then with a flick of her bleached-straw mane, she shook off whatever emotions had threatened to overcome her.

"We'll see what your father has to say about all this," she muttered as she stormed off, only to lurk at the edge of the room.

Whatever was going on behind the scenes, Gemma didn't have time to be distracted by it. She was pleased to see Eli put Morgan in her place, but it wasn't as if anyone was producing any brilliant ideas on how to find her.

Alex had been studying a map of the local area on his laptop before Morgan threw her fit, and he continued to examine it once her tantrum had run its course.

"Ryder is alleged to have killed a man named Edward Bennett after they broke out of prison together. The victim was a career bank robber, and Ryder was a petty thief who ended up in prison for aggravated assault. Bennett's body was discovered a few weeks ago on the banks of the Mertree River." He pointed to a spot on the map.

"What has all that got to do with Gemma?" Bec asked.

"Bennett is reputed to have hidden the proceeds of a number of robberies before he was apprehended and sent to prison. They may have had an agreement regarding the recovery of the stolen money and Bennett ended up dead as a result. My guess is that he died before it was retrieved, and Ryder needs Gemma to locate it."

"Why would this Ryder kill him if he didn't know where the money was? That's ridiculous for a start. And how did he know that Gemma would be able to find it?" Typical Bec, Gemma thought, always two steps ahead of everyone else.

"I don't have either answer. There are multiple theories. One of them is that Ryder has an informant with a personal connection to Gemma."

"Are you suggesting it could have been one of us?" Bec's eyes rested on Morgan.

"I'm not suggesting anything. I'm simply outlining the possibilities. All of you should think carefully about any associations linking Gemma with either Ryder or Bennett. Try to recall whether there has been anyone new in her life recently."

Bec and Deera looked at Eli.

"Anyone else?" No one offered any further suggestions. "Then there's nothing more we can do tonight. I suggest you all go home and get some rest. If you think of anything useful, you have my number. Gemma's parents have been informed, and we'll continue to gather intel from traffic and street cams. If anything breaks overnight, I'll be informed immediately. Be assured we're doing everything possible to ensure her safe return."

CHAPTER FOURTEEN

Alex was met at the front door of a low-set, brick house in the suburbs, by an attractive, middle-aged woman dressed for bed.

"What are you doing up this late Ma? Is Ally all right?"

"Alisha had another bad dream. She wouldn't go to sleep until she said goodnight to you. You shouldn't have to work such late hours when you have a little one who depends on you."

"A young woman was kidnapped tonight." He combed weary fingers through his close-cropped patch of frost. "There are serious concerns for her welfare, but there's nothing else I can do for her right now. I'd better go in and see Alisha. Sorry it's been such a late night. Thank you for everything you do for us."

"I don't mind. I hope there is better news in the morning. Good night my son."

Gemma appreciated the sentiment, but morning would be too late. Her gut told her that her best chance of living through the night was to stay close to Alex.

Having tracked him after leaving the casino by means of his car lights, a soft glow leaking through an open doorway allowed her to follow him into a pastel pink bedroom.

The young girl from her vision the day they had first met, was propped up in bed under a delicate lace quilt. Around her, every available surface was overflowing with the largest collection of dolls and toys she had seen anywhere outside of a department store.

"Daddy—you're home. I've been waiting so long." The child stifled a yawn. "Did you bring a friend with you?"

"I'm alone Ally. I'm sorry I had to work late. Grandma said you wanted to say goodnight to me. Will you be able to go to sleep now?"

The little girl was staring at her. *Listen to her Alex. I'm here.*

"The lady is waving her arms Daddy. I think she wants you to see her. She's standing right beside you."

Alex made a show of checking behind furniture and beneath several stuffed animals. "I don't see anybody baby. You're very tired. Do you want me to stay with you until the lady goes away?"

"Why do you want her to go away? She's pretty, but she's wearing a silly dress." Gemma noticed Alisha looking at the front-splits in her black maxi. "She's pointing at her dress now. It has two big holes in it. You can see both her legs. That's silly." She put her hand over her mouth to stifle a giggle.

"Did Mummy have a dress like that?"

If she hadn't been fighting for her life, the tender scene would have touched Gemma deeply. As it was, she wanted to shout at him.

"Mummy had lots of pretty dresses, but not like that one. She didn't have a shiny silver necklace like the one the lady is wearing either. Why can't she talk?"

Alex's eyes glazed over. Surprise, suspicion, and uncertainty chased each other across his face in quick succession.

"Don't move." When he disappeared out the door, Gemma wasn't sure whether he had been talking to her or Alisha.

He returned with his briefcase and produced a black and white still shot from security footage at the casino. "Is this the lady?"

"Uh huh. She's smiling now. Is she a friend of yours Daddy?"

"Yes baby, she's a friend. Can the lady hear me?"

Alisha looked at Gemma. "She's nodding."

"Does she know where she is?"

"She's pointing to your bag."

Alex removed his laptop and opened the map he had referred to at the casino.

Through an elaborate and time-consuming process of hand signals passed on through Alisha, Gemma guided him towards the area where she was being held captive. With the help of the address, she was eventually able to pinpoint the old couple's farmhouse and a digital dot that lined up with the position of the abandoned building.

"Are you conscious, Gemma?" Alex spoke directly to her, while Alisha conveyed her responses.

"Are you restrained?" They nodded.

"Hands and feet?" Another nod.

"Are you being held in a house?"

The questions continued until he was satisfied that he had determined her exact location and condition.

"I want you to do one more thing for me. Stay with Alisha. Will you do that?" He paused until Alisha responded on her behalf with her assurance.

"Ally, will you keep Gemma company until I get home?"

Gemma smiled at her, and when Alisha smiled and bobbed her dainty head in reply, Alex kissed his daughter on the forehead and raced out the door.

Although the thought of Ryder being alone with her unconscious body terrified her, returning to the shed with him in a rage wasn't an idea she was comfortable with. Despite her dubious relationship with Alex, she accepted that he was her best chance of getting out of the situation alive, and she trusted he knew what he was doing.

"Why can't Daddy see you?" Alisha asked.

Gemma understood her confusion and she shrugged.

"Can I call you my lady?"

That was a new one. She liked it. As far as she was concerned, after what the youngster had done for her, she could call her anything she liked.

Her eyes rested on a framed family portrait on the nightstand. It was the one she had seen in her vision of Alex at the police station.

"That's me and Daddy… and Mummy… before she went away."

The family resemblance was unmistakable. Alisha's mother was a stunning woman, and her daughter was a miniature version of her, with the same silky blonde hair and creamy complexion. And as if to complete the perfect picture, she had inherited her father's striking blue eyes.

Gemma's expression must have betrayed her sadness.

"Don't be sad, Mummy comes to see me sometimes. Daddy doesn't see *her* either."

Having seen her own share of strange phenomena, Gemma knew the visitations were not necessarily the result of an overactive imagination.

"Her name is Ingrid. I hear Daddy and Grandma talk about her sometimes. I'm happy when she comes to see me. She's like you, she doesn't say anything. I wish she could hug me and sing the funny songs she used to sing. I miss her hugs so much."

Gemma promised herself that if she managed to stay alive long enough to meet Alisha in the flesh, she would give her an enormous hug. It wouldn't be anywhere near as special as her mother's, but she would do her best. Her little friend deserved it—and so much more—for what she had done.

Waiting for something to happen was nerve-racking. The tired youngster eventually fell asleep, and Gemma was torn between her desire to know what was happening to her body, and her dread of witnessing something that she would be better off not seeing. Everything hinged on Alex getting to her before the fiery-tempered fugitive decided he had no further use for her.

In the end, the choice was taken out of her hands. As abruptly as she had drifted out of her body, she was drawn back into it, and into the direct path of Leon Ryder's fury.

•••

The foul liquid smelled and tasted disgusting. Gagging and coughing to dislodge it from her nose and throat, she had swallowed some in the process. She didn't even want to think about where it had come from, adding poisoning to her list of potential problems.

"Wake up bitch! I'm warning you, if you start screeching again, that's it. Do you understand?" A malicious scowl afforded Ryder's bearded face an even more sinister appearance in the wavering lamplight. Having revived her by throwing a bucket of putrid water in her face, he stood over her with the empty bucket in his hands.

Her excursion to Alex's house suddenly assumed a dreamlike quality that she couldn't be sure was real.

Scrambling for an idea that would give her a fighting chance, Bec's earlier advice came to mind. It would be impossible to "run away like a frill-necked lizard" with her legs tied, so she tried to remember if any of Daisy's reckless adventures had ever landed her in a similar situation. Had she ever been cornered by a wild beast or caught in a trap?

"Leon," she used his name hesitantly, wary of provoking another outburst.

He glared at her. "How did you know my name? Don't tell me your so-called psychic ability is starting to kick in? It's a bit late now."

"Edward Bennett told me."

A spark of life flickered in his dead eyes. "I always thought you were putting on an act, but the boss insisted you were the real deal. Or is it because you've been talking to the police? I wouldn't mind betting that's more like it."

She had baited the hook, now she needed to reel him in.

She was thinking in fishing metaphors. That wasn't normal, especially since she had never been fishing. All the water she had swallowed must have affected her. Either that, or the blow to her head had broken her brain.

"He communicated with me when I was trying to find your money. That's why I screamed. He's a very scary guy—especially now he's dead."

That part was the truth. He was the scariest thing she had seen since her first CT scan results. "I found the money, and he was trying to spook me—to keep me away from it."

As Ryder's vacuous eyes grew round with excitement, she pictured him swinging on the end of a fishhook.

"That sounds like Bennett, the lousy mongrel. Even now he's dead, he doesn't want anyone else to have it. So where is it? Hurry up and spit it out or you know what will happen."

He clenched his fists, and she questioned if she was doing the right thing. She could be risking another smack in the face—or worse.

"It's not that easy. The money is buried in a state forest. Like I said before, I don't exactly know *where* off the top of my head." She flinched in anticipation of another temper flare. When none came, she continued with her fishing expedition. "I'd need to find the location on a map."

"This better not be bullshit. I can pick a con-job a mile off."

None of Ryder's recent actions led her to believe that he was as smart as he thought he was. He hadn't spotted Edward Bennett's con. Then again, she didn't want to end up like Bennett. He may not have all his switches flipped, but Leon was a vicious killer. His animal cunning was probably the greatest threat to her chances of making it out of there alive.

"There were symbols scratched into a tree. One was a weird hybrid creature. Does that mean anything to you?"

His glassy fisheyes almost popped out of his head with excitement. "He was into all sorts of hoodoo gibberish. I never knew what he was talking about half the time. All right, you proved you're legit."

"Can I check the map? I'm certain I can find it."

"Go on then. Make sure you don't try anything. It's on the table."

When she gestured to her hands and feet, he cut the ties around her ankles, leaving her wrists bound. That was a start, she hesitated to make him suspicious by pushing the point.

As a means of delaying her imminent death, she identified a spot in the middle of the Bellbird State Forest that she thought might work as a backup plan in case Alex didn't make it on time. "The money is buried not far from this building." She pointed to a random structure near a road. "The marks are scratched into a tree in the forest adjoining the property. I know I could lead you to it if I could get close enough."

It was partly true. She was ninety percent sure the money was buried near a tree *somewhere*, and she counted on it being a plausible enough guess to convince him. She tried to sound confident, but her hands trembled as she pointed to the fictional hiding place on the map.

"I'll check it out. If we get there and the money's not there—you're dead."

"It'll be there. I'm positive. Do you promise to let me go when we find it?"

"As soon as I get the money you can go free."

Why didn't she believe him? Aside from the poorest attempt at a sincere smile she had ever seen. There were only two potential ways this would end… and Leon getting the money wasn't one of them.

Outside the shed, he prodded her towards the car by poking her repeatedly in the back with the gun.

"Please don't make me go back in that filthy hole again. The roads are so bumpy and bendy around here… if I get knocked out, I won't be able to help you find the money. I promise I won't cause any trouble if you let me ride up front." As she blundered along in the darkness, she thought about making a run for it.

She could almost hear his brain clunking through the gears as he considered allowing her to ride in the passenger seat. But her discomfort was the least of his concerns.

"You made it here in one piece—you'll live."

When his attention shifted to opening the lid, Bec's advice to run echoed in her head. The words repeated over and over until she couldn't deny their persuasive power any longer. She knew she would be asking for some rough treatment at the very least, but almost anything was worth delaying the inevitable… and it could be her last chance.

Employing her own version of Daisy's daredevil courage—she bolted.

The ground was flat, but rougher than it looked at first glance. Large chunks of bare earth were peppered with tufts of brittle grass, and the whole lot was land mined with coarse rocks and sharp stones.

Guided only by the light of the full moon, and without her arms for balance, she didn't get far before she stumbled. Losing her footing on the patchy ground, one heel buckled under the strain and she almost went down. In a last ditch bid to recover, she lurched three or four strides, but couldn't control her momentum, and in a final bumbling tumble, she crashed face first into the gravel.

Before she could spit the grit from her mouth, he was on top of her. "I warned you to behave yourself. You're going to pay for that." He growled the words so close to her ear, the fumes from his sour breath overwhelmed the reek of his sweat. Grabbing a fistful of her hair, he wrapped it around his scrappy knuckles and dragged her up by it.

The cruel wrench forced a sound from her throat like the howl of a desperate animal. Not only was the pain of her hair being ripped out by the roots more intense than the combination of every needle stuck in her adolescent body over years of medical treatment and testing, but Ryder had dragged her worst nightmares from the pits of hell and brought them to life.

Echoing her tortured screams, the wail of sirens suddenly penetrated the air around them.

When he heard them, Ryder shoved her face back down into the dirt.

Her cheek copped the worst of the impact, but another burst of pain was worth it. Along with the dust in her throat and the grass and gravel on her tongue, she tasted a small amount of satisfaction.

Whatever happened to her, Leon Ryder would be brought to justice.

With the sound of wheels skidding to a stop and sirens fading abruptly nearby, she expected to hear the blast of a gunshot in her ear. Instead, he grabbed her arm and pulled her to her feet.

"Back off or she dies." He pressed the muzzle against the back of her head.

"Ryder...," The sound of Alex's voice sent a surge of emotion through her. "Put the gun down and release the hostage... then we'll talk."

"I'd rather die—and if I die—she dies. Your choice." Using her body as a shield, he dragged her backwards by her hair.

Three sets of headlights illuminated the scene, obscuring the shadowy figures of the police behind a wall of light. Alex's height and build stood out from the rest, and while Gemma trusted him, she was less certain about the other fingers behind the triggers.

Ryder backed away with a grip on her hair and his gun pointed at her head, while the police followed them on foot, weapons fixed on their quarry. She sensed either side may open fire at the slightest provocation and was afraid it was a standoff that wouldn't end well for her.

Just as her dazed brain was weighing the risks of making another run for it, a thumping whack landed in the middle of her back and sent her flying towards the raised guns of the police.

Shots rang out around her.

Trying not to land on her face again—or stagger into the path of a stray bullet—she struggled to keep her balance. Despite her best efforts, it was impossible to stay upright, and she braced for impact as the rocky ground reached out to smash her face one final time. A painful crash landing seemed imminent, when a pair of powerful arms encircled her upper body and delivered her from further facial abuse.

"That was a close call." Alex's dispassionate voice was a soothing balm to her fractured nerves as bedlam broke loose around them.

"I'm OK. You can let me go now," she mumbled. Her mouth was full of grit, and she had trouble catching her breath. Either he was holding her too tightly or she was about to have a panic attack.

"Take your time. There's no hurry." He made sure she was steady on her feet before freeing her arms, then brushed the dirt from her face with the tips of his fingers. "That's better. You've taken quite a beating, but there don't appear to be any deep cuts."

She ran her hands lightly over her face and head to feel for damage, yelping when she touched the bump where she had connected with the hard floor. That one was going to hurt for a while.

The absence of gunfire gradually infiltrated her damaged skull, and she whirled around to check the vicinity for further threats.

"No need to worry. The site is under police control," he reassured her.

"What happened to Ryder?" She shuddered at the thought that he may have gotten away.

"He shoved you as a diversion before escaping into the bushes. He was wounded. It's only a matter of time before we get him."

Her heart sank.

CHAPTER FIFTEEN

"Good morning. How are we feeling now?"

The hovering nurse's cheery greeting was both pleasant and somehow irritating. Gemma couldn't justify that much positivity so early in the morning, especially so soon after her most recent excursion to the gates of the torture realm and back.

"Is my mother here?" She had a vague recollection of being admitted to Clear Lakes Research Hospital well after midnight, and her mother watching over her until the early hours of the morning.

"Sorry darl, she left a couple of hours ago. I'm Lily." The nurse pointed to her name badge. "I've been on the ward since you were brought in last night. You were pretty out of it by the time you got here."

Lily took her temperature, measured her blood pressure and noted the readings on her chart. "Your doctor will see you when he does his rounds. He'll let you know the results of the tests they did in emergency. I don't want to jump the gun, but if they're all clear and he's happy you don't require any further tests, you should be able to go home after he sees you. Is there anything you need in the meantime? Do you have any pain?"

"Now that you mention it, I do have a pretty bad headache."

"It's no wonder. Judging from those bruises, you've been through the ringer, haven't you? Do you want me to get you something for the pain? Are you allergic to any medications?" She frowned as she studied Gemma's chart.

"Not that I know of." She had been subjected to so many drugs over the years, anything was possible.

When Lily moved on, Gemma scrambled out of bed and flexed her limbs to feel for signs of other injuries. Her relative lack of discomfort was surprising, and if Ryder was behind bars, it would all have been worthwhile.

A shower, toilet and tiny vanity were squeezed into a compact space attached to her room. There was a mirror above the basin, and when she saw her reflection, a shocked gasp escaped her swollen lips. It was no wonder Alex had been careful when brushing the dirt from her cheeks. She looked like she'd gone a couple of rounds in a boxing ring and then been dragged along on her face for good measure.

"Knock, knock." It was her mother's voice.

Her whole family was waiting for her in the main room.

Lucas didn't try to hide his enthusiasm when he saw her. "Holy crap! Someone really did a number on you. Sick."

"Lucas," her father growled.

"Does it hurt darling?" Her mother had dark circles under her eyes, and Gemma knew it would have been a rough night for her as well.

"Not too bad. It could have been a lot worse." She climbed back into bed.

"Don't fret Kris, she'll be her old self again in no time."

"I've got a splitting headache actually," Gemma complained, stung by his breezy certainty.

"Not everyone can shrug off a traumatic experience as easily as you can Doug."

The combination of worry and lack of sleep had made her mother irritable.

"I didn't mean to appear indifferent. I was trying to cheer her up. Have you spoken with the police this morning, Gem?"

"No Dad, I haven't seen anyone except a nurse."

"We won't pester you with a lot of questions. We'll wait until you're feeling better. We've been worried sick about you and just wanted to make sure you weren't hurt too badly. Your mother is going to wait here until you're discharged. Then she'll bring you home where we can take care of you. We assumed that's what you'd want."

"That's perfect. Thanks Dad, I'm sorry to put you to so much trouble."

"You don't have to be sorry about anything. It's not your fault some maniac tried to kidnap you. We've been to your apartment and your mother put together a bag of things she thought you might need. Lucas and I will drop in again on our way home to pick up the big guy."

"How's Bones? Did you feed him?" She had forgotten about him until her father mentioned him.

"I didn't have much choice. He nearly chewed my leg off. One night without food won't hurt him. He could stand to lose some weight."

"Lucas! What do you think you're doing?" Her mother's voice was shrill.

Everyone jumped, including Lucas.

"I have to get a shot of Gem's face before we go. It's too cool. It would go viral for sure. My mates won't believe how beat up she is."

"How about we rough you up as well little dude? Then you can tell them how it feels." Bec had slipped into the room behind him. "Or you can take a selfie instead." She ruffled his hair with both hands as he ducked out of her way.

She was followed closely by Deera and Lucky.

"We're off then." Her father kissed her on the forehead and patted her mother on the shoulder. "See you two at home."

"I'll walk out with you and give Gemma a chance to catch up with her friends."

Deera's hand flew to her mouth when she saw Gemma's face. "Thank the goddess you are in one piece. You *are*—aren't you?" She gave her the once over to make sure all fingers and toes were accounted for.

"Nothing too serious. Cuts and bruises mainly."

"You should not have left the cocktail lounge alone. I should have gone with you. It's all my fault."

"Don't be absurd," Bec said, "it's nobody's fault. Everyone should have taken the whole stalker thing more seriously. We might have to keep her on a leash in future."

"Sorry about the drama. It's all good, I promise. What happened after you figured out I was missing?"

"I saw you take off during my performance. Thanks for the boost to my ego by the way. When you didn't come back, and Deera hadn't heard from you, we knew something was wrong. We spotted your phone on the floor of the garage, and when you weren't in your car, we called your detective."

"He's not *my* detective." She cringed at the idea things had come to that.

"The camera feed from the gaming floor is the only one closely monitored by security," Lucky explained. "Once the police became involved, they checked recorded footage from other parts of the casino." He had worked enough jobs at the Meridian to know how the surveillance measures worked.

When they got to the part in the story where Eli told everyone Morgan meant nothing to him, Bec couldn't contain her enthusiasm. "I wanted to smack that loser so bad… but there was a police officer in the room, so I thought I'd better not push my luck. It was almost more satisfying watching Eli shatter her delusions instead."

Yes, it was, Gemma thought.

"I think he really likes you. You should have seen how angry he was at Morgan. I'm sure he is very relieved that you are safe." Deera was a born romantic. She couldn't help herself.

"I don't know. I haven't heard from him."

Bec had been rummaging through the bag Gemma's mother had packed for her. "There are cosmetics in here. You should tidy up a bit. It will make you feel better. Your face could do with some TLC… and those hospital PJs aren't exactly a great look either."

Her candid comments did nothing to cheer Gemma up and she was tempted to follow the advice. Anything would be better than looking like a reject from a zombie movie.

"Is it a bad time?" Everyone looked around to see Eli standing in the doorway. "I can leave the flowers and come back later." He was holding the biggest bunch of sunflowers she had ever seen.

"Speak of the devil…," Bec said. "We were on our way out anyway. Come in and make yourself at home."

Lucky and Deera took the hint and said their goodbyes, and Bec gave Gemma one last sly wink as she followed them out.

"Thank you for the flowers. You didn't need to do that. They're beautiful. How did you know I love sunflowers?" She tried to distract herself from thinking about how repulsive she looked.

"I noticed the ones in your apartment yesterday and guessed you liked them. I wanted to tell you how sorry I am… for last night at the casino… and earlier."

She blushed at the memory of his abrupt departure from her apartment.

"It was hardly your fault I was kidnapped."

After she said the words, she acknowledged to herself that she *did* think it was slightly his fault.

"I feel bad about what happened between us, and for any part I may have played in what you went through last night. I treated you poorly and you have every right not to forgive me."

It was hard to stay angry after such a sincere apology, but she couldn't help a little moral outrage. "You lied to me from the start, and I trusted you."

"I understand if you want nothing further to do with me."

"Why don't you tell me the *real* Eli Nite story. Then I'll reassess how much of an apology you owe me."

"That sounds fair, especially since you know most of it anyway. For the record, I was going to come clean yesterday at your apartment. Then if you remember, I became a little distracted, and all coherent thought flew out the window. I kept picturing you in bed after your nightmare and couldn't get the image of you wearing that revealing lingerie out of my head. I got carried away in the heat of the moment. Can you forgive me?"

"I pushed you away… and you backed off. You stood up for me against Morgan last night too. Thank you for that."

"You heard about that debacle, did you? I assumed the way Morgan behaved in the cocktail lounge was part of the reason you walked out. I was angry at myself for not stopping her foolishness earlier, but I didn't want to spoil Bec's performance for everyone. I don't know how I would have reacted if the situation had ended differently. I can't even guess what you must have been through."

After hearing Eli's explanation, she felt a little ridiculous about the way she had reacted—both at her apartment—and the casino. "Let's start over," she offered.

He reached for her hand and held it in both of his. "It's wonderful to see you again after all these years Gemma. I only wish it was under different circumstances."

When his fingers stroked the palm of her hand, a sensual spark ignited under her skin.

"I neglected to tell you earlier, that following high school, I studied criminal justice at university. Afterwards, I worked my way up in private security, and then a short time ago, I was appointed national security director for Centian Corporation—the company that owns Palm Gardens Lifestyle Village."

"Where's your father these days? I remember seeing him at some of your football matches. Does he still work in Aurora Waters?"

"My father is based in Sydney. I know it sounds like nepotism, but he nominated me for the position at Centian." With her hand still in his, he drew back to arm's length and looked her up and down, as if seeing her in a new light. "You attended my school football matches? Now there's something I would never have expected."

"Your father is your boss then?"

"One of them, yes."

She got the idea there was a lot more to the story than he was letting on, and she still didn't understand Morgan's connection with his father.

"Then I assume your *business trip* back to Aurora Waters has something to do with Frank Malloy's disappearance from Palm Gardens?"

"I'm sorry I couldn't tell you the truth about that earlier. Freda Meyer contacted me the day after Frank went missing. She said he had left the village Friday afternoon, telling staff he was visiting a relative and would return in time for the evening meal. When he hadn't arrived back by the next morning and couldn't be contacted, she asked me to make discreet enquiries to determine whether it was necessary to inform the police."

"And you thought I was involved in some way?"

"Not really. Procedure required that I check into a report by a staff member that you had been asking questions about Frank. I needed to find out what you knew, without alerting you to my investigation. I'm sorry. I thought it would mean some tactful questions over dinner, with no harm done. The whole thing turned into a bit of a shambles."

"Welcome to my world."

He took her hand again and pressed it gently between both of his. "In some ways you're as fragile as a butterfly Gemma. You're also strong when you need to be… and caring… and sometimes too reckless for your own good. You're a fascinating woman, and I'd like the opportunity to get to know you better, if you'll let me. Is there a chance we can start over? I didn't intend to hurt you, but I understand if you're unwilling to trust me again."

Before she had time to fathom everything he'd told her, there was a knock at the door.

Alex cleared his throat. "Sorry to interrupt, but Gemma and I have some loose ends to tie up."

Eli brushed a few wayward strands of hair from her face with his fingertips, and she wasn't sure if the awkwardness she felt was due to his open demonstration of affection in front of Alex, or sensitivity at her less than glamorous appearance.

"I'll get out of your way Detective. Thank you for what you did last night. I can't tell you how relieved I am that Gemma is safe."

"Gemma did most of the hard work." Alex's eyes bounced off hers before returning to their usual frosty restraint.

"When we parted ways at the casino, the outcome didn't look promising," Eli looked at them in turn, evidently waiting for further information. "Things must have changed a great deal in a short time."

"Luck played a big part. An anonymous tip came in after we left the Meridian."

"Gemma must have a guardian angel. It's hard to believe we could have gotten that lucky. What about Ryder? Has he been located yet?"

"With the injury he sustained, it shouldn't be long before we track him down."

"Did you need to speak to me Detective Vannen?" The conversation was making her uncomfortable, and she hoped Eli would take the hint.

He acknowledged her less than subtle dismissal with an almost imperceptible nod. "You two must have a lot to discuss. I'll leave you to tie up all those loose ends."

He raised her hand from where it rested on the bedcovers and pressed it to his lips, drawing her eyes to his. The longer he maintained eye contact, the more she expected an unsettling image to flash across her starstruck eyes. Thankfully, her mind remained blissfully vision-free.

"If you're willing, we'll continue our chat when you're feeling better." Releasing her hand, he turned to Alex on his way out. "I would appreciate an update on the Malloy case when you have time."

Eli's departure was a relief, which she put down to the fact that she was tired, and her head hurt. She wasn't in any condition to cope with so many confusing issues at once.

"It looks like you're in pretty good shape, considering what you went through."

"You don't look too bad yourself… I mean… because you didn't get much sleep last night. Mum has dark circles under her eyes."

"Is that what you meant? I thought you might be feeling the effects of all those blows to the head." She could have sworn the corner of his mouth quivered.

"Probably," she admitted.

"A few solid hours are all I need. I'm used to it. As soon as I knew you were admitted to hospital, I had no difficulty falling asleep." It was the most informal disclosure he had ever made about himself.

"Has there been any sign of Leon Ryder?"

"Nothing has turned up so far. He should have been apprehended by now, particularly with a gunshot wound to the upper body. Someone must be helping him."

"And you're telling everyone you found me through an anonymous tip? Is that what really happened?"

"I couldn't very well say you magically appeared in my daughter's bedroom and passed on your location through a series of charades."

It sounded so bizarre she almost laughed. "No one would ever believe it anyway. At least the mysterious anonymous informer gets us both off the hook. I still don't know if I believe it. At the time I thought I may have been more *psycho* than psychic."

"Have you ever done anything like that before?"

"Nothing exactly like that—no. That was a first."

"How resourceful of you. I suppose life-threatening situations can sometimes teach us things about ourselves we would otherwise never have known. The experience taught me something too." His piercing eyes focused intently on hers. "I learned I shouldn't underestimate you. I'm intrigued as to how you managed to show up at my home, or how you knew where to find me for that matter."

"A lot of trial and error. Once I figured out how to do it, it was pretty simple. It's all about the light."

"That's as clear as mud. You're either incredibly lucky, or cleverer than you would have anyone believe."

"Thanks for the vote of confidence."

"Alisha has been pestering me about you since she woke up, and I've been debating how best to respond to her questions. I expect it's somewhat of a risk, but I brought her to meet you. She's waiting outside with your mother. Do you mind?"

"Of course not. I don't know what I would have done without her help. I owe her a lot."

"Alisha told me about her new friend," her mother said when Alex ushered them into the room. "It sounds like you two have a bit of catching up to do."

"It's *my lady*," Alisha squealed when she saw her. "Daddy, it's my lady. Can you see her?"

"Yes Ally, I can see her. Why don't you say hello?"

"What happened?" she asked in a shy little voice. "Did somebody hurt you?"

"I fell down, that's all. Can I give you a hug?"

Gemma's composure was almost destroyed when the affectionate child flew into her arms. Tears spilled from her shadowed eyes and rolled down her battered cheeks onto the starched, white sheets.

"Don't cry, you're safe now. Daddy saved you, didn't he?"

"He did. He's very brave—a real hero."

"I couldn't have done it without you, baby. You were the one who really saved Gemma, I mean *my lady*." He bowed and Alisha giggled, wide-eyed and adoring.

Gemma compared Alisha's bravery to her own actions in the face of recent challenges. "You're a hero too, Alisha. When I feel better, I'll show you how much I appreciate what you did for me. I'll take you out for ice cream, would you like that?"

The little girl batted long, thick lashes at her father. He nodded, and her doll-like face was instantly enthusiastic. "Yes please, I really, really love ice cream, especially chocolate."

"I need you to wait with Mrs. Glass, baby. My lady and I have work to do." He stroked her platinum hair and dropped an airy kiss on her forehead. "I'll take you home shortly." Opening his laptop, he turned to Gemma. "Are you ready to do some work, *my lady*?"

Alex's repeated use of Alisha's nickname for her, alleviated a little of her anxiety at the prospect of further cross-examination. "Go on then… I'm as ready as I'll ever be."

Instead of firing questions at her as she expected, he read a description of the kidnapping from his laptop—beginning at the point Ryder ambushed her and ending with her rescue. It was written as if *she* had described it to *him*.

"If you agree with what I've drafted, I'll print it and you can drop into the station and sign it later, when you're up to it."

"Won't anyone be suspicious about the anonymous caller… or the reason I was taken?"

"You would be amazed at the number of investigations that are solved through anonymous tips. People don't want to get involved—as you well know."

She flinched. "Ouch! You don't have to rub it in. I've learned my lesson."

"If there is an enquiry, it won't be an issue. As to why you were targeted, we have you on record as saying you had no idea why Ryder was trying to kidnap you. Would you like to change your previous statement?"

She couldn't believe how easy he had made things for her. "But should you do that… leave stuff out I mean?"

"If you insist on telling a different story, I can't stop you."

Thinking about it, the approach made sense. "No one would believe the truth anyway."

"Also, Alisha would be dragged into the investigation, and that's the last thing I want. Well? Will I use the written statement I prepared, or do I need to make some changes?"

"Use the version you've already written… and thanks."

"I'm glad you're happy with my proposal. Now if there's nothing further, I have a lot of work to do."

"There is one other thing." It was an impulsive decision.

"Yes?"

"I haven't thanked you properly… Alex."

"Since when are you calling me Alex?"

"For a while now—behind your back. Do you mind if I call you Alex to your face?"

"As long as it remains private. I wouldn't want anyone to think we have a personal relationship."

"Of course not. What I wanted to tell you is that I don't think a simple thank you is enough after what you did. I owe you more than that."

"You don't owe me anything Gemma. I was doing my job. What are you trying to say?"

She was glad the cuts and bruises on her face would camouflage the sudden explosion of heat in her cheeks. "I meant I would look at the photos of Frank's crime scene for you. I might be able to help find his killer."

She sensed his confusion. "The department would be grateful for any assistance you can provide. Although considering your initial response to my request, are you sure you want to do that?"

"It's the least I can do. When I needed help, you were there for me. It's only fair I do something in return."

"If you're offering, I won't say no. Additional insight could prove valuable. We'll arrange it when you come in to sign the statement."

When Alex left soon afterwards, Gemma and her mother settled in to wait for the doctor. The last thing either of them expected was an unwelcome visitor.

"What do you know, somebody left a pair of glasses sitting around. A pair of *Glasses*—get it?"

Would the torment never stop? Being trapped in a room with Morgan Payne was like being taken hostage all over again. One experience like that was enough for a lifetime.

"What are you doing here Morgan?" her mother said, the lines around her mouth deepening further in her already drawn face.

"Hello Mrs. Glass, I'm very well thanks, how are you? Definitely in better shape than someone else we know. Isn't that right?" She smirked at Gemma.

"After what she's been through, it's a miracle she survived at all, let alone escaping with superficial injuries. It could have been a lot worse."

Her mother was sticking up for her against the school bully again, and Gemma wanted them both to know she could fight her own battles. "You should see the other guy. I doubt he'll be kidnapping anyone else for a while."

"That's what you say. It must feel good to be noticed for a change. I bet you haven't had this much attention in years."

Nan was right, Gemma thought. The black hole Morgan called a brain showed zero signs of intelligent life. She didn't want to talk to her, but if she was going to face her demons, she had to start somewhere.

"Mum, would you mind grabbing me a coffee please? I could do with a caffeine hit right about now."

Her mother screwed up her eyes as though she was having trouble with her vision. "If you're sure that's what you really want. I'll be back in a minute." She looked pointedly at Morgan.

"What are you doing here?" Gemma asked once they were alone.

"I wanted to see how you were with my own two eyes. I heard you had a rough time last night, and I had to be sure you weren't badly hurt."

Even without the sarcastic tone, it was clear Morgan had come to the hospital for a reason, and Gemma knew it wasn't in concern for her welfare. "Why are you really here? Get to the point or get out." She was too tired for games. Where were the police when she really needed them?

"No call to be rude, but if you insist… I wanted to see for myself what all the fuss was about. You could have got those bruises from walking into a door for all anyone knows."

She spotted the sunflowers on the bedside table and grabbed the envelope attached to the wrapping. "How interesting… and ugly," she said as she removed the card. "I never did like sunflowers. I wonder who they're from? Mummy and Daddy, the hottie policeman, or somebody else?"

After reading the message, she focused spiteful laser-eyes on Gemma. "I'm wise to you—you little wannabe. I know what you're up to and you won't get away with it. You might have all your gullible friends believing your fairy tales, but I know the truth… and soon everyone else will too."

Morgan had always been an overbearing tyrant, but her usual snarky attitude suddenly reached a whole new level of vindictiveness. After dangling the card within Gemma's reach, she pulled it from her grasp at the last second. Then waving it in the air in front of her face, she tore it in two, before dropping the pieces onto the floor.

CHAPTER SIXTEEN

By Monday morning, the bumps on Gemma's head had softened from rock hard golf balls to spongy marshmallows. The scrapes on her face had dried to form an assortment of crusty scabs, and her bruises had faded to less vibrant versions of their previous thundercloud hues. Thanks to the magic of concealer, she was able to cover the worst of her war wounds with makeup.

"I swear Bones has put on a couple of kilos over the weekend," she complained to Deera, who had volunteered to help carry her things up from the garage.

As she set the chunky ragdoll's crate down on the floor inside her door, she picked up a piece of paper from the tiles.

"So much for a warm welcome home." She wanted to scream with frustration. Someone had pushed a note under her door while she was away, and her first impulse was to crumple the hateful message and toss it in the bin.

"Let me see." Deera plucked it from her hand. "Oh no. You should call Detective Vannen. This isn't funny."

"Exactly what I need, another reason to speak to the police." She didn't want to ask for Alex's help again so soon.

"What's wrong Gemma?"

"What makes you think something is wrong?"

"Then why are you calling?"

"Maybe I wanted to tell you that I moved back to my apartment… or thank you for coming to my rescue the other night… or that someone slipped a threatening note under my door."

"Threatening in what way? What does it say?"

"You're a lying fake…" Her voice faltered as she read the words aloud, "and you deserve everything that's coming to you."

"I'll be there as soon as I can. Stay where you are, and don't answer the door to anyone until I get there." Alex's tone carried an unexpected note of urgency.

"You should move back to your parents' house," Deera said. "It would be safer."

"I don't think it would make any difference where I sleep."

"Then you should carry a security device of some type. A personal alarm or pepper spray would be better than nothing. Lucky can show you many ways to protect yourself. I'll ask him to drop by when he finishes work."

"You're right," Gemma said after they tossed around a few ideas, "I should be more proactive. I can't afford to sit around and wait for disaster to strike. If Leon Ryder is still out to get me, I'll be more prepared next time he makes a move."

Her heroic intentions and bold words sounded convincing, but when a loud knock startled them, she almost jumped off her stool with fright.

Deera was sympathetic and attempted to suppress a giggle, but neither of them could resist laughing at her absurdity. Every time one bout of hilarity subsided, another spurt of laughter set them off again.

A louder and more insistent knock followed, by which time Gemma was on the brink of losing it completely.

Charging to the door, she released the latch and ripped it open, mentally daring the person on the other side to step over the threshold and try to harm her.

Alex stared at her open-mouthed, as if he had forgotten what he was about to say or couldn't bring himself to utter the words. When he finally spoke, his voice was measured and controlled.

"It could have been anyone on the other side of that door. I dropped everything in case Deera needed help to keep you calm. I thought you were on the verge of hysteria, not enjoying a practical joke. Is there some sort of illicit substance at work here that I should be aware of?"

"Not unless adrenaline is illegal." She muttered the words into her chest, studying the floor with sudden interest. "We… I… got a fright when you knocked. It broke the tension and made us laugh, that's all."

Alex's mouth was set in a grim line, and she gave up on further efforts to explain, holding out the note to him like a chastised schoolgirl. "You had to be there. I'm sorry, it must be the stress."

"This is no laughing matter. Do you have any idea who it's from?" After reading the words that were intended to turn her into a nervous wreck, he had slipped back into interrogation mode.

"Leon Ryder is a given, although he doesn't strike me as the literate type. The only other person who comes to mind is Morgan."

"Why would you suspect Morgan Payne? Despite her immature disposition, don't you think that would be going too far, even for her?"

Gemma reached into a drawer and pulled out the card that Eli had given her. After taping it back together, she had read the message countless times and knew the words by heart. It wasn't the sort of message she wanted to share with anyone, but under the circumstances she didn't have a choice.

"On Friday morning, Morgan came to the hospital to see me. She opened an envelope addressed to me, took that out and read it, then tore it in half and threw it on the floor. She babbled something about knowing what I was up to—whatever that means—and stormed out."

She handed it over, thankful when Alex didn't embarrass her any further by remarking on its contents.

"That explains why you believe she's involved. Has anyone else touched either of these notes?"

Deera raised her hand.

"I'll have them both dusted for fingerprints. The one with the tape may prove to be a challenge. We'll see what we can pull from it. I'll need both of you to supply a sample of your prints so we can eliminate them."

"Are you going to question Morgan?"

"First I'll request a sample of her prints."

Good luck with that, Gemma thought.

"Anyone else?"

"I can't think of anyone—unless it's someone connected to Ryder. You said he may have an accomplice. Maybe it's them."

"I don't recall ever saying that in front of you. I mentioned him having help after he was shot."

She didn't want to explain about eavesdropping at the casino, so she improvised. "I thought that's what you meant."

"Do you have any clairvoyant insight into who slipped it under your door?"

"I didn't hold it for very long." Her encounter with Edward Bennett had dampened her enthusiasm for embarking on another psychic fact-finding mission involving dangerous criminals. "But I suppose if I'm going to check out the other photos, it makes sense to include the note."

She held out her hand and Alex returned it to her.

After imprinting the sinister words onto her retina, they jumbled together in the darkness behind her eyes, and the shadows created by the blurry letters combined to form a fuzzy likeness.

"Whoever it was, they were dressed in baggy clothing, and wore a cap and sunglasses. It could have been anyone, so I guess that was a waste of time."

"That's a shame. We've been checking Ryder's known associates, but nothing has come to light. We could have used a break. Now he's in the wind the investigation has stalled. Brass are inclined to make the search for Frank Malloy's killer the top priority."

"I can understand that." She didn't like it, but she agreed it made sense from a police perspective.

"Are you prepared to make good on your promise?"

"Did you think I would chicken out?" He must have a poor opinion of her if he thought she would go back on her word so easily.

"I was providing you with an opportunity to change your mind. I have a selection of crime scene photos with me, as well as the formal statement that I read out to you at the hospital. It's ready for your signature. I thought I would tie up all the loose ends while I'm here."

When he fanned the photos out on the kitchen bench, Gemma heard a sharp intake of breath. She had been so wrapped up in her own thoughts, she had almost forgotten Deera was still in the room. Her squeamish friend had retreated in horror from the gruesome sight.

The shots of Frank's body—positioned the way she had seen it in her vision—tempted her to withdraw her offer. The possibility she would witness the elderly man's suffering had been playing on her mind, and she needed to call on all her newfound good intentions to mentally revisit the scene of the crime.

After leaving her trance state a few minutes later, an insidious shiver snaked its way up her spine.

"Can I see the rest of the photos?" she asked, cautiously optimistic that her observations may provide new insight.

Alex conjured them like a magician, slapping them down on the bench. "Did you discover something useful." His normally bulletproof expression revealed a hint of excitement.

The expectation in his voice was contagious, feeding her desire to be right about her suspicions. The thought that she may have uncovered valuable information almost made up for the stress of seeing poor Frank's abused body again.

"Were the cable ties used on Frank Malloy compared to the ones used in my case?"

"Both are in evidence under different case IDs. Any viable DNA and fingerprints will be run through the national database. Further forensic tests can be requested if you believe the cases are connected."

"They look identical to me. And not only that… Frank was tied up *exactly* like Ryder tied me to the chair inside that old shed. Arms, legs, hands, feet—they were all positioned exactly alike. That couldn't be a coincidence, could it?"

"I can request a forensic comparison of the ties and try to speed up the DNA results. If a match is made, the investigation into Ryder's crimes will be back on top of the list. I suppose I don't need to advise you to be careful. Have you thought about taking additional safety precautions?"

"We were discussing that very topic right before you knocked on the door." She smiled at Deera.

"I won't pretend to know what you two find so funny, just as long as you're taking the threat seriously."

"I am—very seriously. I intend to do whatever I can to protect myself. Do you have any suggestions?"

"Not opening the door to strangers would be an appropriate place to start. There are a number of free personal safety courses available. It's a question of finding one that suits you. Eli Nite's experience in the security industry may prove beneficial. Now I come to think of it, your employer would be another excellent resource. He has a reputation in the surveillance industry for the use of hi-tech gadgets."

She hadn't thought of Harvey. His agency contracted all sorts of security specialists. She made a mental note to talk to him about it the next time she saw him.

•••

"I'm glad you called," Eli said when she phoned him later in the day, "I've been thinking about you, and I was worried I would never hear from you again."

Left to her own devices, she wasn't as confident as she pretended to be. She could have used additional moral support from Alex, but between his work and family commitments, she understood he didn't have time for one more responsibility. The way Eli had spoken to her at the hospital, and the message he had included with the flowers, had spurred her to call him.

"I've been thinking about what happened," she confessed, "and a lot of it wasn't your fault. You did say to let you know if there was anything else you could do."

"Anything. How can I help?"

"With Leon Ryder still out there somewhere, I've decided to upgrade my personal security to a slightly higher level than non-existent. Can you spare the time to offer some suggestions?"

"Would you like to discuss it over dinner?"

"That sounds like a better alternative to staying locked inside my apartment for the rest of my life. No after-dinner walks this time though. How about somewhere quiet, where we can talk? Preferably somewhere Ryder can't find me."

The consequences of their last outing were still fresh in her memory, but if she was going to take a risk, then a date with Eli would be one worth taking.

"I know another restaurant you'll love. It's out of the way, the views are incredible, and the food and wine are first class. Now I'm fully aware of your precarious situation, I pledge to keep you safe."

Although she was no longer in possession of Eli's card, his words were indelibly etched in her memory. After weighing every syllable countless times, she was in no doubt that her next encounter with him would be a romantic date.

Dearest Gemma,
I never intended to hurt you. All I ask is the opportunity to make amends by earning your forgiveness. You are more important to me than you will ever know.
Love Eli.

CHAPTER SEVENTEEN

Freda Meyer marched out of her office and intercepted her as she signed in at Palm Gardens reception. "I'm so glad I caught you Gemma. Could you spare me a moment please?"

Aside from pushing her out of the way, it appeared she had little choice. The manager had her boxed in.

"Eli Nite informed me that you've been assisting the police with enquiries into Mr. Malloy's death."

The implied disapproval touched a sore spot with Gemma. She usually fought the urge to throw a military style salute whenever she ran into the village manager, but this time a different hand gesture came to mind. Her frosty attitude was uncalled for and she was sick of it.

"Frank was Nan's friend. When no one did anything to find him after he went missing, she asked for my help."

"Everyone here is devastated, naturally. I'm sure it won't be long before they find the person responsible. You do understand that no one could have done anything to prevent what happened?"

"My family rely on you to make sure my grandmother is safe. If something ever happened to her because your staff don't care, or aren't paying attention...," the words hung in the air like balloons about to pop.

She leaned in and lowered her voice. "We had no reason to believe Mr. Malloy was in any danger. He informed staff he intended to visit a family member. Residents do that sort of thing all the time. There was no way we could have known."

It was true they had no way of knowing, but Gemma couldn't help thinking they should have done more. "If you had brought the police in sooner instead of trying to sweep his disappearance under the rug, he might still be alive."

Freda's eyes darted around the foyer. "I appreciate your concern for your grandmother, but don't try to insinuate that Palm Gardens staff are in any way answerable for Mr. Malloy's death. We did absolutely nothing wrong and bear no responsibility whatsoever." She thrust her ample chin into the air.

Gemma couldn't be bothered wasting any more time going around in circles. She had her own ideas about how to ensure her grandmother's safety, and she left the manager to wallow in her excuses. Aside from keeping a closer eye on Nan in future, she intended to speak to Eli about Morgan.

As though her thoughts had somehow conjured them, the individuals in question miraculously appeared in the corridor connecting the main building with her grandmother's unit block.

"What a pleasant coincidence." Eli turned hard eyes on Morgan. "Thank you, Morgan. You can go."

"Hang on a minute, we haven't finished talking. You didn't answer my question." Her voice wound down like a sputtering engine grinding to a halt.

"The answer is no. Gemma and I have personal business to discuss. If you'll excuse us, we would appreciate some privacy."

Morgan tossed brittle hair back over her shoulders. She had no intention of giving up so easily. "I don't know why you want to spend time with a sickly thing like her. I suppose you feel sorry for her."

For once there was no sting in her juvenile remarks, and Gemma swatted her away like a harmless stink bug. "I'm glad you finally get it Morgan... you'll *never* know... because you're clueless. So, get lost."

"You need to teach me your technique for getting rid of her. I don't seem to have the knack."

"It's a useful talent I recently acquired. Glad you appreciated it. If she's such a pain—pun intended—why don't you fire her?"

He hesitated for a split second before answering. "She works under the direct authority of the board. My father hired her, and only he or the board can terminate her employment. Let's forget about her. Are you on your way to see your grandmother?"

"I wanted to see how she's coping with the news of Frank's death. I haven't seen her since they found his body."

"I knew you wouldn't mind if I introduced myself. We had quite the conversation about you."

The amusement in his eyes threatened to destroy her composure. "You can't believe everything Nan tells you. I'm worried she's going slightly senile. She tends to exaggerate things—*a lot.*"

"I admit I was enthralled by some of the more personal details she revealed about you." He rested the palms of his hands lightly on top of her shoulders and stared into her eyes. "We're on a first name basis now you know. She must have thought I was a trustworthy sort of character, to divulge all that intimate information."

Although she knew he was teasing, heat blasted across her skin. At least she hoped he was teasing. Knowing her grandmother—anything was possible.

He bent his head to hers and whispered in her ear. "Do *you* trust me, Gemma?" The intensity behind the question surprised her.

"There are no more reasons why I shouldn't… are there?"

As if to reassure her of his sincerity, he pulled her to him.

Her brain alerted her to the inappropriate time and place, but the rest of her body made no attempt to disengage. When he pressed his lips against hers, she was immediately transported to a secluded haven, where they were blissfully alone in the moment—until they weren't.

"That was unexpected," she said after he released her.

"Are you referring to my impulsive gesture or the untimely arrival of that staff member?"

"Both, I guess."

"Get used to it. That encounter is definitely *to be continued.*"

The weather forecast predicted the possible chance of a thunderstorm later that evening, and she could already feel the electricity in the air. Every nerve ending was buzzing as she attempted to pack her hyperactive hormones on ice in preparation for the visit with her grandmother.

"I should get moving then, I wouldn't want to be late for dinner."

"I look forward to picking up where we left off," he said as she walked away.

Suddenly, a few short hours felt like far too long to wait before seeing him again.

Nan was expecting her, and usually welcomed company with open arms, but when Gemma knocked on her unit door, there was no answer.

Curious as to where she might have gone, she called her mobile.

To her surprise, it rang inside the unit, so she tested the door handle and discovered it was unlocked.

Nanna Glass was forgetful occasionally, but it wasn't like her to be careless with security.

Letting herself in, she found her grandmother's phone and purse lying on top of the polished wooden cabinet where she stored her fancy glassware. Once the phone stopped ringing, the only other sound inside the empty unit, was the forlorn tick of the pendulum clock on the living room wall.

Calling out as she went, she checked the rest of the unit to make sure she wasn't lying helpless in one of the other rooms. She didn't venture into the bedroom very often, but a dark stain on the beige carpet beside the bed looked out of place, and she doubted her finicky grandmother would leave a mark like that untreated.

A dab of her finger revealed that it was damp.

Gemma had spent enough time in hospitals to know what fresh blood looked and smelled like, and her internal alarm bells jumped straight from yellow alert to full blown air raid siren.

Without thinking things through, she took the first course of action that sprang to mind and raced back to reception, only stopping along the way to ask if anyone had seen her grandmother. No one had—at least not for a few hours—and she couldn't help thinking about what Leon Ryder had done to Frank.

There was only one woman behind the reception counter, and she was on the phone. When Gemma tried to speak to her, she raised her index finger and slanted her body to discourage further interruptions, all while keeping her eyes fixed firmly on her computer screen.

Frustrated at the delay, she checked Freda's office.

Finding it empty, she was about to phone Eli when Morgan flounced into the foyer.

"What's up Gemini? Did your cat get run over by a truck? Or was it *you* that got run over? That would explain the hair." Her gurgled laughter sounded even more sinister than usual.

Gemma didn't feel like putting up with her caustic personality, but she needed information. "Have you seen Nan?"

"What if I have? Why would I tell you anything?"

She should have known better than to expect a direct reply. "If you're not going to be helpful—then go away. I'm busy."

"Busy trying to find Gloria? You're looking in the wrong place."

"What do you mean? Have you seen her or not?"

"You sound upset." The words dripped with honey-coated venom. "She left with a man I've never seen before. I assumed he was a friend of hers. They were heading for the car park."

"How long ago?"

"You're getting a bit full of yourself lately my girl. If you don't speak more civil, I won't tell you anything."

Gemma tried to maintain her composure for her grandmother's sake, despite wanting to shake the answer out of Morgan. "Please tell me how long ago you saw her leave the building."

"That's better. Amazing how polite you can be when you want something—isn't it? They left just before you started barking at me. If you hurry, you might catch them."

She couldn't believe Morgan had kept her talking so long while her grandmother had been leaving the village. Not wanting to waste any more precious time, she took off at full speed in search of her and her mysterious companion.

There were two dozen car spaces in front of reception, and when she didn't find them there, Gemma hurried to her own car and drove in turn to each of the other parking areas scattered throughout the complex.

Scanning the roads and grounds as she went, a few times she slowed down to take a closer look at a familiar crop of dense silver hair or gaudy leisure suit. None of which turned out to be her grandmother. If she had gone with someone to one of the car parks, she wasn't there now, and odds were, she was no longer on the grounds.

During her trek back to reception, she worked through the possibilities. No matter how many innocuous reasons she thought of to explain her grandmother's disappearance, none of them made any sense. It wasn't like her to leave her unit unlocked with her valuables still inside… or to go out when she was expecting a visitor. There was also the disturbing question of the blood.

She considered contacting her mother and father, but concluded it was only postponing the inevitable. The lesson she had learned from the Frank Malloy catastrophe, was to act sooner rather than later. Even if Nan was safe, she had to find out where she was.

Sprinting back to the unit, she let herself in and headed straight to the bedroom.

The shock of finding her grandmother's velour-clad backside—wiggling in time with the motion of cleaning the bloodstained carpet—was like a physical blow to her gut.

"Nan, where have you been? I've been running around like an idiot trying to find you."

"I was only away for a few minutes."

"Why did you go out and leave your door unlocked with your phone and purse still inside?"

"I didn't mean to frighten you. I knocked my arm on the bedside table. It started to bleed, so I went down the hall to see Dot. You know how fragile my skin is these days. I ran out of band aids, and she has enough first aid supplies in her bathroom cupboard to stock an ambulance."

Gemma thought how paranoid she must appear to her easy-going grandmother. She had overreacted because of the note. The threats to her life had caused her to jump to the wrong conclusion. Even to her own ears, she sounded like she was coming unhinged. She would never have flown into such a panic if the same thing had happened two weeks earlier.

Morgan's lies hadn't helped either.

"I'm sorry for giving you the third degree. When I saw the blood… and you left all your things here."

"I knew you were going to be here any time, so I thought I would leave the door unlocked for you. And to tell the truth, I forgot all about my purse. You know what Dot's like, once she gets talking there's no way to shut her up unless you knock her over the head with her walking stick."

"On the bright side, she did a great job on your arm," Gemma acknowledged. The damage was covered by a neat bandage. "Here, let me do that."

She helped her grandmother up off the floor and took over cleaning the bloodstain from the carpet. She was furious with Morgan. The pouting piranha had been lying through her teeth the entire time, and she made a mental note never to believe a word she said in future.

Pretending the stain was Morgan's deceitful face, she would have enjoyed scrubbing it into oblivion, but thought Nan probably wouldn't appreciate it if she wore a hole in her carpet. Once she calmed down, she warned her grandmother about Morgan's vindictiveness, and how she had sent her off on a wild goose chase.

"I've known the truth about that little vixen for a long time," she said after Gemma explained what had happened during her absence. "I don't fall for her childish games. I'm sorry the so-and-so sucked you into one of her lies. I'm going to lodge a formal complaint with Freda about her… not that it will make any difference."

"I think I underestimated her. I'm beginning to wonder how far she would go to get back at me."

"She hasn't managed to get the better of me in all this time, I don't intend to let her start now. If a dirty big global virus couldn't get me, then a little local germ like Morgan Payne has no chance."

"How are you coping with the news about Frank?"

"It's very upsetting. Poor Frank had a lot of happy years left in him. When you get to our age, the loss of friends and relatives is an unfortunate fact of life, especially with all the dreadful new diseases spreading around the world these days. But it's hard to accept something so needlessly cruel and vicious. I think I'll retire from euchre now that he's gone. It won't be the same without him."

"Why don't you dedicate the competition to Frank's memory? He wouldn't want you to stop playing, especially when you enjoy it so much."

"The Frank Malloy Memorial Euchre Tournament. That's a wonderful idea. He would love it. That way, his memory will live on in the village forever." Her eyes misted with tears. "Thank you, sweetie."

She pretended to assess the bandage on her arm while she composed herself. When she eventually turned to face Gemma again, her mischievous smile had returned. "I almost forgot… that handsome Eli Nite came to see me the other day. Why didn't you tell me he was your boyfriend? I almost died of shock when he spilled the beans. You need to keep me up to date on these things. You wouldn't want me to have a stroke, would you?"

"He said what?"

"That you went out to dinner with him. He likes you—you like him—he's practically your boyfriend. You do like him, don't you?"

"A lot has happened since I last saw you. How much have Mum and Dad told you about what's been going on?"

"When I mentioned young Eli, your mother seemed to think something was cooking between you two. She wasn't certain how serious it was—but if the description of the flowers is true—he's smitten. How do *you* feel?"

"There have been a lot of misunderstandings between us, and he won't be in town for long, so I don't want to make a big deal of anything."

"That's a pity. Men like him don't come around very often. Anyone who goes to the trouble of introducing himself to your gorgeous… if slightly more senior grandmother… is definitely a keeper." One of her sharp eyes squinted in what Gemma assumed was an attempt at a cheeky wink. "Between him and that Detective Vannen I had the pleasure of speaking to during the week, it's been one cutie-pie after another around here lately."

"It's hard to believe it's just over a week since Frank went missing."

"Your mother said the friendly detective got to you in the nick of time the other night. I'm glad I didn't know about it until afterwards. How are you feeling? You're still pale, except for that whopping bruise on the side of your face."

Gemma touched her cheek, self-conscious that the bruise remained so obvious. She would need to apply a heavier coverage of concealer before dinner.

CHAPTER EIGHTEEN

Someone was at the door. It was either Lucky—there to give her security tips—or Eli was early. Opening it a crack, she left it on the chain.

"Has something happened to Nan?" She eyeballed the Palm Gardens manager through the gap.

"Your grandmother is perfectly fine. She was winning loads of goodies at bingo when I left."

"If there's nothing wrong, then why are you here?" She didn't have time for more of Freda's plausible deniability rubbish.

"Your grandmother made a complaint about Morgan's conduct earlier. I wanted to offer my sincere apologies. May I come in?"

"I'll call you tomorrow to arrange a better time. I'm on my way out soon."

"I'm flying to Sydney early in the morning to attend a conference. It would be in all our best interests to sort this out before I leave."

Gemma didn't want to let Nan down, but something didn't feel right. "Thanks for letting me know. I'll make sure to keep an eye on her while you're away. Call me when you get back and I'll drop by to see you."

"Morgan and your grandmother had a disagreement after you left," Freda blurted. "Morgan threatened her over the complaint and I'm afraid the situation will get out of control if I'm not there to keep her in line."

Furious at the thought of Morgan making threats against her grandmother, Gemma opened the door.

Before she could stop her, Freda barged into the apartment and Rose Honeycomb slipped through the door behind her.

Rose dropped a duffel bag at her feet and pointed a gun at her.

Gemma looked from one to the other, not fully grasping what she was seeing.

The dithering lifestyle coordinator removed a fistful of cable ties from the duffel bag and passed them to Freda. "Tie both hands to something solid in the kitchen. Make sure she's not going anywhere in a hurry. Then find the bathroom and lock yourself in. If you come out before I leave, or if I hear a sound out of you, you'll get this." She waved the gun in her face.

Freda looked like a lump of butter melting under hot lights as she took the ties and slipped into the kitchen.

Gemma stood her ground, convinced she had either landed in a parallel dimension or was trapped in another nightmare. She searched the faces of the two women for clues that it was all an elaborate charade. "What's going on? Is this a joke?"

Beads of perspiration dotted Freda's brow, but Rose's angular face was carved from stone.

Rose glared at her. "Don't you know? I thought you were psychic."

"Is someone forcing you to do this? The police can help. Let me make a phone call and we can sort this out."

Mention of the police detonated the blood vessels in Rose's face. "All you had to do was tell Leon where the money was buried. There was no need for the police to become involved. Now get over there or I'll shoot you." The scarlet spiderweb spread like wildfire under her pasty skin. "I should shoot you anyway, as payback for Leon. First your leg, then your arm, then something more lethal."

As she aimed the gun at each of Gemma's body parts in turn, her eyes glittered red-hot through a mask of pure hatred.

Get help! Gemma mouthed the words at Freda when she joined her in the kitchen.

The manager's response was either a mimed apology… or a sign that she was about to wet herself. With the amount of perspiration pouring from her face, it was hard to tell. Either way, her reaction wasn't promising.

Without saying a word, she used one tie to bind Gemma's wrists. Then with a convoluted concoction of twists and turns that would have made a Girl Scout proud, she used several more to secure her to a cabinet door handle. When she was done, she took off down the hall.

Hearing a door slam, Gemma turned her attention back to Rose. "I tried to find the location of the money for Leon, but he didn't give me enough time. It was too well hidden."

"Why don't you just admit it?" Rose said, pacing back and forth in the living area while Gemma kept an eye on her from behind the breakfast bar. "All that bragging by your silly grandmother was a lie, and your website is a con. I should have known. Leon tried to tell me."

"If you let me go, I won't say anything to anyone. I'll try to find the money for you. I could try right now."

"I don't care. Don't you understand? You had your chance. It's too late now. There's nothing left for me anymore."

Shambling footsteps made their way down the hall, before stopping abruptly outside the apartment door. Gemma considered calling for help but didn't dare risk it with the gun aimed at her head.

They waited, with neither of them making a sound as a succession of knocks followed. Gemma clung to the breath in her lungs as if it could be last air she ever breathed.

When the footsteps eventually moved off, she said, "That's a friend of mine. He's a security guard. He'll be back, or he'll call the police. You should get out of here."

"All the more reason to kill you now then."

"Why would you want to kill me? All I've done is try to help you."

Rose's hand clenched around the grip of the gun. "I want to see you suffer, the way I suffered when Leon died."

She tried to disguise her relief that Ryder was dead. "The police shot him. I didn't see what happened. I didn't know he was dead. I can find the money for you if you give me more time."

Rose shot thunderbolts of rage at her through stormy eyes. She was grief-stricken and bitter, a dangerous combination. "It's too late. Weren't you listening? Don't you understand? Leon is dead because of you." Her voice was shrill, and the gun wavered as her muscles contracted. "After I've taken care of you, I'll get rid of that meddling grandmother of yours too—running around asking questions about Frank Malloy—she's as bad as you are."

At the threat to her grandmother, a surge of adrenaline fogged Gemma's brain. She tested the strength of the cabinet handle, regretting her decision to blindly follow orders. She could try to pull the door from its hinges, but not while Rose was aiming the gun at her.

"I'm sorry the police killed Leon. I've always liked you Rose. We might have been able to work something out if you had just asked me."

"There's no way you would have helped us voluntarily. You're wasting time." She reached for the duffel bag.

"You were always so kind to Nan…"

When she hesitated, Gemma took a shot at encouraging her tendency to indulge in mindless chatter. "How did someone like you get mixed up with Leon and Edward Bennett?"

"Oh, all right, I'll let you stew in your own juices a few minutes longer. I was an administrator at the prison where Leon and Ed did time. Ed agreed to share the stash from his robberies if I helped him escape. He tried to double-cross us… and Leon killed the good-for-nothing liar."

While she spouted her evil monologue, Gemma's mind raced to find a way to derail her plans.

"With Ed dead, we didn't think there was any chance of recovering the money, until we learned that Frank was his grandfather. I took the job at Palm Gardens to get close to the old man, but it was all for nothing in the end… thanks to you and your grandmother. Happy now?" she smirked.

Gemma had hoped the explanation would take minutes—not seconds. "Don't blame Nan," she pleaded, "she had nothing to do with any of this."

"I'll take it easier on her—how's that? She won't suffer as much as you. Some tragic accident is all it takes. It happens to elderly people all the time."

"Why kill anyone? Why kill Edward Bennett… or Frank? You're not a murderer. It's not too late to change your mind."

"If Ed kept his part of the bargain, none of this would have happened. Leon wasn't supposed to kill him. He lost his temper. And it wasn't *his* fault Frank had a weak heart. You can thank your grandmother for your part in all this. You were our last big chance, but you turned out to be useless. You were the biggest mistake of all. It's because of you that I've lost Leon forever. It's only fair that you should suffer."

"You can still walk away. You haven't killed anyone. The police know it was Leon who caused Frank's death."

"Do they?" The look in Rose's eyes was as barbarian as her eyebrows. "Well, aren't you full of revelations after it's too late. Where was all this information when we needed some of it? Sounds like it only comes out when it suits you. My life is ruined. I've lost the only man I've ever loved. You can suffer for the rest of yours—as short as it's going to be."

She was acting like a lovesick teenager out for revenge, and Gemma wondered why no one at Palm Gardens had ever noticed she was unhinged. Then again, with Morgan on staff, her personality probably seemed relatively normal in comparison.

Whenever Gemma's attention gravitated towards the duffel bag, her imagination ran wild. The fate the fiendish Juliet had planned for her sounded like it would take longer than a gunshot wound to the head. Was there an axe in there? She couldn't be that sadistic, could she?

Rose reached into the bag. But instead of an axe, she produced a scarf. And after gagging Gemma with it, she raised the gun to her head.

It was all happening too fast. She wasn't prepared.

There was a click… and her heart stopped.

The mad woman hacked up a grisly laugh. "It's not a real gun, you moron. It's a toy. Close enough to the real thing to fool someone as gullible as you, though."

She had barely recovered from the shock when her phone rang.

"Someone's trying to call you." Rose zipped across the room. "That's enough chit chat. It's time to get down to business." She locked the sliding door to the balcony and dropped the key into her pocket. Any hope that she was bluffing went with it.

"We need to be security conscious—don't you think? I'll make sure to lock the front door behind me on my way out. When Freda finally wakes up to what's going on, it'll be too late for the both of you. Daft cow. No great loss there either."

While she was distracted, Gemma leveraged one foot against the cabinet door and tugged with all the strength she could muster. The ties and handle remained rock solid, and she regretted not making more effort with the weights at the gym. Her wrists were raw from pulling against her restraints and she had nothing to show for it.

That's what she got for renting an apartment with such an old-fashioned kitchen. Her grandparents had been right. Things really were made to last back in the good old days.

Rose reached into the duffel bag and swapped the bogus gun for a small jerry can. "If you don't stop that racket, I'll slit your throat before I set the place on fire." Unscrewing the cap, she splashed some of the contents over the curtains on either side of the balcony door.

The pungent smell of petrol wafted across the room, and as it seeped into Gemma's lungs, the sickeningly sweet scent inflamed her defiance. Stealth mode had failed miserably, so she caught hold of the cabinet handle and pounded the door against the frame, banging it as loudly as she could.

"We can play it that way if you like. I'll slit your throat and have done with it. Is that what you want?" She set the jerry can down, hurtled into the kitchen and plucked a carving knife from the block next to the stove.

Shocked into self-preservation mode, Gemma ducked as she lashed out at her with it, yelping when the sharp blade connected with her jaw. Uncertain how much damage the knife had inflicted, she felt something warm and wet trickle down the side of her neck.

She debated whether to test her luck further, imagining herself knocking the knife out of Rose's hand with one foot, while simultaneously clobbering her in the head with the other. Once she was flat on her back, she would pin her to the floor with a scissor lock and force her to cut the ties.

"I take that vacant stare to mean that you intend to behave yourself. Just as well, we're almost ready for the bonfire."

Gemma snapped out of her fantasy at the reference to her impending fiery doom. No matter how much she would like to have Daisy's skills, she didn't have the strength or agility necessary to get the better of Rose when she was trussed up like a chicken prepared for the oven.

As an alternative, her desperate brain sifted through the scenarios of every action movie she had ever watched in search of an escape plan that didn't require brute strength, a tunnel, a car chase, or a bomb. When nothing even remotely realistic came to mind, she wasn't sure what else to do.

Giving up was never an option. She had promised her grandfather that she would take care of Nan, and in turn he had promised to be waiting for her when she was ready to join him. It suddenly occurred to her that she had nothing to worry about.

She trusted him and refused to believe that this was the end. Knowing she wasn't ready to join him yet, her muscles relaxed.

Rose struck a match, the flame burst into life, sputtered… and then died. Snapping it between her fingers, she flicked it away.

Gemma's heartbeat slowed.

A second match was struck, and again the tiny spurt of heat and light was extinguished before it caused any damage. In a fit of annoyance, Rose dumped the spent match on the floor, stomped on it, and ground it into the rug.

Rose didn't have a chance against her grandfather, but Gemma kept a close eye on her just in case the angry wasp changed her mind and decided to slit her throat instead.

But she wasn't about to give up on her diabolical plan so easily. After checking the doors and windows to make sure they were all shut tight, she cupped her hands to protect the next match from non-existent gusts of air… and this time it ignited.

She tossed it at the curtains, and as the flimsy synthetic fabric whooshed into life, she turned triumphant eyes on Gemma.

The moment she opened her mouth to speak, a terrifying howl cut her off, reverberating eerily inside the enclosed space, before climaxing in a haunting crescendo. The sound came from behind the curtains, and while Rose's mouth remained wide open, whatever she was about to say was lost in the ensuing mayhem.

Gemma watched in awe as Bones exploded from his regular hiding spot and scaled the one thing that stood between him and safety. Climbing until he couldn't go any further, his razor-sharp claws dug into the flesh of Rose's back and shoulders as she spun in frantic circles in a frenzied attempt to shake him off.

Against the fury of her efforts to remove him, he clung like a leech to her head, with his claws fully extended and anchored in the skin of her face and skull. In the heat of battle, his moaning wails increased in volume and pitch, until the combination of his hellish screeches and Rose's excruciating shrieks sounded like someone was being tortured with a band saw. The harder she tried to remove him, the deeper his claws went.

In a final desperate bid to be free of her feline scourge, she tripped over the coffee table and plunged headfirst into the burning curtains.

The agile ragdoll jumped away as soon as his climbing post began to topple, shooting like a bullet towards the bedroom.

By the time Rose righted herself it was too late, her clothes were already alight. Still screaming, she flew through the apartment door—a raging fireball—with blood pouring from her head and back.

Gemma watched the curtains disintegrate under the searing flames, dissolving like cotton candy in the mouth of a greedy child. Once they were consumed, the fire sought new fuel around the window frame. Heat blasted her from across the room while a cloud of smoke billowed from their decimated remains. The noxious monster crawled across the ceiling and descended over her in a veil of carcinogenic toxicity.

When the smoke alarm finally kicked in, its shrill beeps were a deafening distraction from the possibility of becoming a human marshmallow.

Where in the aftermath of the demonic apocalypse was Freda? Why didn't she come out of the bathroom? The cat-versus-crazy duel was over, but it wouldn't be long before she would be on fire, or dead from smoke inhalation.

She thought she had heard somewhere that more people died from asphyxiation than burns, and to protect herself, she pulled the neck of her t-shirt up over her nose and stooped as low to the ground as possible. The smoke was so thick by that stage, she couldn't see anything, and she prayed Rose had left the door open in her hurry to flee the flames.

CHAPTER NINETEEN

"Is anybody in there?"

Gemma slammed the cabinet door repeatedly, drawing Lucky to her like a wraith in the haze.

"I'll get it—watch out." Reaching over her, he gripped the edge of the door with both hands.

He heaved, it jerked, and there was a cracking sound. That was the end of one hinge, and his sledgehammer arms moved in for another assault. The second hinge gave way with the crunch of metal against metal.

"Come on, I've got you." He hoisted her over his shoulder and carried her along the hallway and down the narrow stairs, with the cabinet door dangling awkwardly from her wrists, and banging against the walls as they passed. Setting her down on the front lawn, he removed the gag and used it to stem the dribble of blood from her jaw.

"Thank you so much." The words croaked from her mouth between coughs. "That was close. I can't believe you got me out."

"Sorry about your door. I didn't want to waste time when I could hardly see. Deera is gonna skin me alive," he groaned, "what a bloody mess."

"She'll forgive you for getting a little blood on your uniform. And don't worry about the door. You could have knocked down a wall and I wouldn't have cared. You saved my life."

"I wasn't talking about your actual blood. That's no problem. She left a message for me to go see you as soon as I finished work. When you didn't answer the door, I walked away. She wasn't home, so I ate a snack instead of checking on you. She's definitely gonna kill me."

"I'll stick up for you. I'm only alive thanks to you."

"I should try to help with the fire. There could be someone else trapped in the building."

Freda had slipped her mind in the panic. "Go on. I'll be OK. You better check my bathroom if you can get to it. There could be someone in there. Be careful, I don't want to have to explain to Deera if anything happens to you."

She watched Lucky bolt back inside the building, surprised how fast he moved for someone his size.

It reminded her of Bones. The last time she had seen him, he was a ball of fur, streaking towards the bedroom. She tried to remember if he was on fire. The thought that he hadn't made it out of the burning apartment in time hit her like a bomb. Her precious boy could be dead or severely injured, and she was tempted to go back inside to look for him.

Eli emerged from the crowd of people and vehicles beginning to congregate in the street and driveway. "What happened? You're covered in blood. Are you hurt?" He crouched down on the grass beside her.

"I'm much better now you're here." It took a moment to register that he was there to pick her up for their date. She tried to smile, wincing instead at the sting of the cut on her jaw. "Rose Honeycomb tried to slit my throat and burn me alive. Nothing unusual when you consider everything that's happened this week. We'll have to take a rain check on dinner."

"What on earth is going on with Palm Gardens? First Frank Malloy is killed, now Rose Honeycomb tries to murder you. Do you know why?"

"She was Leon Ryder's girlfriend—slash accomplice. You really need to evaluate the hiring policies at that place. I'm going to ask Nan to find somewhere safer to live."

He skimmed soothing fingers along her grimy arms. "I guarantee everyone and everything at the village will go under the microscope. I'll talk to my father. Do you trust me to look into things?"

That was the million-dollar question. Did she trust Eli enough to ensure her grandmother's safety? Whenever she was around him, she felt like she was enveloped by a protective cocoon, inside which nothing could harm her or the ones she loved.

Alex's height and hair stood out like beacons among the congregation of onlookers and service personnel swarming the area.

"How badly are you hurt?" he asked when he reached them. "Have the paramedics examined you yet? I need to take your statement when you're up to it."

"Make up your mind Detective. Do you want me to tell you how badly I'm hurt? Or do you want to get my statement first? Or should the paramedics check me out while you take my statement? I can't deal with an interrogation right now—to be honest. What are you doing here anyway?"

There was blood all over her… the ridiculous cabinet door was still attached to her wrists… and all he wanted to do was question her.

"I take that response to mean that you're handling your most recent life-threatening confrontation in your usual stoic fashion. To answer your question—I'm immediately advised of any police situations that arise in connection to an ongoing investigation. Also, your friend called me. I believe he was running back into a burning building at the time."

The previously militant stare in his eyes had tapered to amused tolerance. "I didn't mean to overload you. I'm eager to hear your version of events. However, there's no hurry. I was trying to say that your physical well-being is a priority. It didn't come out the way I intended. Whenever you're ready is perfectly acceptable."

She couldn't be sure, but it sounded like he mumbled the words "my lady" under his breath.

"I'll survive. I'm just stressed as hell. Would you like to get this thing off me please?" She acknowledged to herself that she may have overreacted as she raised her wrists to highlight the fact the cabinet door was still attached.

"My apologies, I should have done that first. I thought I might need these." He pulled a small pair of wire cutters from his jacket pocket, removed the ties from her wrists and sealed them inside an evidence bag. "We found more cable ties in Rose Honeycomb's bag when we searched it, along with the replica handgun. You seem to have defended yourself adequately, considering you were restrained. I'm intrigued as to how you managed to get the better of her… though given her wounds, I can hazard a guess."

A fresh-faced paramedic joined the group. "Sorry to interrupt, but I should take a look at that laceration."

"Do you need me to stay Gemma?" Eli had received a phone call while she had been busy with Alex. "There are matters that need my urgent attention, given that two Palm Gardens employees are involved."

"You know about Freda?"

"They found her stuck in your bathroom window frame. She was trying to squeeze through when she became wedged, and only called for help after the smoke alarm went off. Your friend came to the rescue. She's safe, if somewhat embarrassed."

"Could you check on Lucky for me… and find out what happened to Bones. He took off like a rocket to my bedroom after he made mincemeat of Rose."

"From what I've seen of your friend, he can take care of himself. And if Bones is anything like his owner, I'm guessing he's fine too. I'll let you know as soon as I find them."

Alex made his excuses next, after advising her that he would return shortly to take her statement. He took the cabinet door with him to secure as evidence, executing a barely perceptible bow before he walked off.

The friendly paramedic helped Gemma to her feet and guided her to the back of one of the ambulances. "Now we're alone, can you help me assess you by answering some easy questions?"

"Just what I need, more questions."

"I'll try not to grill you like a detective," she joked, as she wrapped a blood pressure cuff around Gemma's arm. "Symptoms can develop up to thirty-six hours after exposure to the effects of fire. Are you having any problem breathing?"

"Not as much as I would have been… if that knife had sliced through my jugular instead of my jaw."

"You'll get a thorough examination when we take you to the ER, and probably a few stitches. I'll clean and dress that wound so it doesn't get infected. You don't need any more problems by the looks of you. You've really been through the wars lately, haven't you?"

"It's been a rough week. Did you see what happened to the psychopath who started the fire?" She needed to know Rose wasn't about to come after her again.

"Some members of my team are treating a woman for burns and a vicious animal mauling. She won't be going anywhere except to a hospital under police escort. There's no need to worry about that one for a while. You got off easily in comparison."

"With what she had planned for me, I'm thanking my lucky stars. Speaking of luck, have you seen a big guy in a security uniform anywhere?"

"He's hard to miss. He's been giving the fire brigade a hand. From what I hear, he had the blaze contained by the time they got there. If there's anything left of your apartment, I'd say it's him you need to thank."

Tears pooled at the rims of Gemma's eyes in reaction to the young paramedic's unguarded words.

"Sorry, that came out wrong. Are you insured?"

"It's not that. It's... the last week has been one hairy carnival ride after another. If things hadn't worked out the way they did... if I didn't get out of there when I did..."

"Do you have somewhere to stay?"

The question made her think of her parents and she wondered if anyone had contacted them. "I can move back home with my family. Do you know what happened to my phone? I should probably call them."

"I'll check if anyone has seen it if you like. You're welcome to borrow mine to make the call."

"Thanks. It can wait." That was one call she wasn't in a hurry to make.

"Here you are. We've been looking for you." Deera rushed up and threw her arms around her. Lucky and Bones were with her.

"Thank you so much for looking after Bones. I thought I might never see him again after what he went through." She couldn't believe there wasn't a smudge of ash on his fluffy cream coat.

"Don't worry. I think he still has all nine lives left," Lucky said, setting Bones' crate down at her feet.

"My hero." Deera entwined both her slender arms around one of his bulging biceps.

"I think that *vicious* cat of Gemma's is the real hero." His shoulders bobbed up and down with suppressed laughter.

"Let's say he was the first hero on the scene, and you were the second. I don't know how I'll ever be able to thank you."

"I guess it was your *lucky* day," he grinned, kissing his adoring wife on the forehead as she gave his arm another affectionate squeeze.

Gemma smiled. It really did feel like her lucky day. Despite her apartment being trashed, she was oddly optimistic. She wasn't sure if a long-term relationship with Eli was feasible, but she was comfortable with the possibility.

"I have more good news," Lucky told her. "When I went back to your apartment, the fire had burned itself out. I never saw anything like it. Everyone is giving me the credit, but I didn't do too much."

"Really? I can't believe it. I thought for sure it would be a write-off."

He brought a sunflower out from behind his back and presented it to her.

"Is this one from the bunch Eli gave me?"

"I thought you might like it," he said, placing it in her outstretched hand.

The moment the vibrant flower touched her ashen skin, a shroud of deathlike cold settled over her. Above her head, the hazy twilight sky plunged into darkness, and with the appearance of a shocking vision, her worst nightmares were manifested in the shape of an unexpected face.

Her grandfather had been right. There was someone who needed her help. A powerful force was trying to manipulate her… and she was the only one who could stop it.

•••

Donovan Nite surveyed Sydney Harbour from a lavish office, high above the streets of the North Shore.

"The plan is still on track, regardless of the last stage not going as well as anticipated. Something unforeseen must have impacted her fear levels dramatically. The situation should have pushed her to the limit."

While he listened to the response of the person on the other end of the call, he reached out and snapped a head from one of the giant sunflowers overflowing from the ornate crystal vase on his desk.

"There are no happy endings… only meaningful ones. The girl would have lost her battle years ago if not for the intervention of modern science. She should be grateful for the generous gift of additional time. We're making her life significant when it would otherwise have remained completely ordinary. Could there be a more praiseworthy pursuit?"

He paused again to hear the reply.

"Keep in mind that the board needs to see results, otherwise they'll move on to more lucrative projects. There could be vital information we're missing. Our man has been working on another psychic barrier. It should prove more reliable in managing her increasing abilities. Keep up the excellent work and we'll have what we need in no time."

Ending the call, he crushed the flawless petals between his fingertips and flicked the remains into the rubbish bin beneath his desk.

D.C. Walsh is a poet, fiction writer, and author of The Sunflower Connection. A lifelong fan of all things supernatural, the themes of her fantasy mystery novel combine her love of nature with her fascination for unexplained phenomena. An ex-serving member of the Australian Defence Force, Bachelor of Science (Psychology) graduate, and amateur photographer, her diverse interests and experience provide a wealth of inspiration for her creative pursuits. Her human family and two fur children also generate the occasional idea or two. A clairvoyant once predicted that if she ever started writing she would never stop. While that revelation turned out to be one hundred percent accurate, whether the remainder of his predictions come true—only time will tell.

CPSIA information can be obtained
at www.ICGtesting.com
Printed in the USA
LVHW031250151221
706194LV00004B/302

9 781685 831400